BEYOND THE PEAKS OF PERIL...

... there stretches from the shores of the great sea of Sogar-Jad a mighty plain. Under the eternal noon of Zanthodon observers might have perceived a strange and unusual party traversing this grassy immensity.

In the first place, the party consisted of a herd of dinosaurs. . . . In the Underground World, of course, the sight of the monster reptiles was commonplace, for it is here in the vast cavern-world beneath the Sahara that survivors from forgotten ages have lingered on hundreds of millennia since the last of their kind vanished from the Upper World.

The first things that was surprising was that the immense bronze-and-copper-colored dinosaurs wore bridles, bits and reins.

The second thing was that men were riding on their backs. . . .

"With a thunderous hiss, the enormous serpent lunged at Hurok . . ."

HUROK OF THE STONE AGE

Lin Carter

Illustrated by
Josh Kirby

DAW BOOKS, INC.
Donald A. Wollheim, Publisher

1633 Broadway, New York, N.Y. 10019

FIRST PRINTING, FEBRUARY 1981

1 2 3 4 5 6 7 8 9

 DAW TRADEMARK REGISTERED
U.S. PAT. OFF. MARCA
REGISTRADA. HECHO EN U.S.A.

PRINTED IN U.S.A.

Contents

IV.   THE DIVINE ZARYS

V.   THE THUNDER-WEAPON

VI.   GODS OF ZAR

LIST OF ILLUSTRATIONS

This book is for my friends
Art Saha and Matthew Saha,
George Townsend, Smita Pai,
and Roy Squires.

THE STORY THUS FAR

When the Yankee adventurer Eric Carstairs let the distinguished scientist Professor Potter hire him to find the entrance to mysterious and legendary Zanthodon, a gigantic cavern-world below the Sahara, neither could possibly have anticipated what they were getting into.

They discovered that, over innumerable ages, the tropic warmth of the Underground World had provided refuge for a remarkable number of unexpected survivors from the remote past . . . stalwart tribes of blond Cro-Magnons, hulking and apelike hordes of Neanderthals, monstrous dinosaurs of every description, as well as beasts from the Ice Age such as the woolly mammoth, the dreaded sabertooth tiger, and the mighty cave bear.

As well, certain survivors of other cultures had taken refuge in this prehistoric world: not only the rapacious and cruel Barbary Pirates, but cunning and decadent survivors of age-wrecked Minoan Crete, the original Atlantis of legend.

Befriended by the brave and gallant Cro-Magnon tribes, Eric rescued and fell in love with the beautiful cave-girl, Darya of Thandar, and when she was carried off by enemies, he and his friend the old scientist joined her brawny sire, Tharn, High Chief of Thandar, in the search. Along the way the warriors of Thandar met and joined forces with another Cro-Magnon tribe, the men of Sothar.

Many and terrible are the beasts and cunning foes the searchers after the lost princess encountered in their quest. But perhaps the most terrible of these adversaries were reserved for the last.

The Barbary Pirates, driven from their Mediterranean fortress-base generations before, had fled to the steaming seas of Zanthodon, retaining their mastery of the high seas. When the lustful Redbeard, captain and prince of the corsairs, car-

11

ried off Darya to his island-citadel, the Cro-Magnons found it beyond their abilities to pursue them, as they not only had no notion as to the whereabouts of the pirate kingdom, El-Cazar, but lacked the ships to get there.

Another disaster befell when Eric Carstairs and the Professor, having strayed from the Cro-Magnon host in their wanderings, were taken captive by the men of Zar, the Scarlet City, a surviving colony of Minoan Crete.

These astounding people from the past, scions of one of the most advanced of the nations of antiquity, tamed even the mighty dinosaurs of this primitive jungle with their mastery of weird telepathic crystals. It seemed an impossible task for his friends to follow Eric Carstairs and the elderly scientist into the great metropolis of Zar; nevertheless, a small band of his former companions, including Hurok the Neanderthal, attempted it, unwilling to evade their responsibility to the man who had done much to free them from their ancestral heritage of constant warfare and suspicion of strangers.

For Eric Carstairs was the first man to make friends with one of the beastlike Neanderthals, and was responsible for ending forever the hostilities which had formerly existed between every tribe or nation in Zanthodon. He taught his new friends the value and meaning of cooperation, tolerance, and brotherhood—hard lessons to absorb in this savage wilderness, where roam titanic beasts from Time's remotest dawn in a hostile world filled with trackless jungles, vast plains, impassable mountains, thundering volcanoes, and uncharted seas.

Join Eric and his comrades now as they experience the ultimate of the marvels and mysteries preserved from the wreckage of the past in unknown Zanthodon, the Underground World.

—LIN CARTER

Part One

---◆◇◆◇◆---

DRAGONMEN
OF ZAR

Chapter 1 ___

THE DRAGON-RIDERS

Beyond the Peaks of Peril there stretches from the shores of the great sea of Sogar-Jad a mighty plain. Under the eternal noon of Zanthodon observers might have perceived a strange and unusual party traversing this grassy immensity.

In the first place, the party consisted of a herd of dinosaurs. Now, on the surface world this would indeed have been remarkable, as the last of the great saurians of the Dawn perished into extinction long before the first true men evolved from their marsupial ancestors. Here in the Underground World, of course, the sight of the monster reptiles was commonplace, for it is here in the vast cavern-world beneath the Sahara that survivors from forgotten ages have lingered on hundreds of millennia since the last of their kind vanished from the Upper World.

While our hypothetical observers would not have found the giant lizards remarkable, in themselves, there was that about them that would have astonished.

The first thing that was surprising was that the immense bronze-and-copper-colored dinosaurs wore bridles, bits, and reins.

The second thing was that men were riding on their backs.

Now, the dinosaurs of Zanthodon come in two distinct varieties. One is the mighty predator, savage, ferocious, hungry—terrible fighter of unkillable vigor.

The second variety are the more placid and amenable herbivores, slow-witted, ruminative, and no more to be feared than we fear dairy cattle. Even these last, however, have never been broken to saddle—not because of their ferocity for they lack any, but simply because their intelligence is too rudimentary for them to learn to obey commands. As well, they are virtually walking stomachs, and must eat constantly in order to fuel their gigantic carcasses.

15

I could not identify the species of dinosaur into which the harnessed monsters may best be classified—if my learned companion, Professor Percival P. Potter, Ph.D., ever named them for me, I am afraid that I have forgotten—but I can assure you that these stalking monstrosities were huge beyond belief.

As for the men on their backs, there was nothing particularly remarkable about them, except that they represented a species of humankind I had not yet encountered here in the Underground World. There are the hulking and hairy-chested Neanderthal men (the "Drugars," as the folk of Zanthodon call them), and the tall, lithe, blond and blue-eyed Cro-Magnons (or "panjani"), plus a surviving remnant of Barbary Pirates fled here when the fleets of Europe were scouring the Mediterranean to crush the corsairs and eliminate their depredations on shipping.

But beyond these, the Dragonmen, as the folk of Zanthodon seemed to call them, were unique. Small, slim, olive-skinned, with silky black hair and flashing black eyes, dressed in high-laced sandals and abbreviated garments of fine linens dyed yellow or scarlet or blue, they obviously were the children of a higher order of civilization than any I had yet encountered in this fantastic subterranean world—with the possible exception of the pirates.

They lived in a land called Zar, I had been given to understand, which lay inland from the coast, far to the "east." I call the direction "east" because it is a convenient term; actually, here far below the world where the steamy skies are perpetually illuminated by weird phosphorescence there is no way to tell one direction from another. If you will think about this for a moment, you will realize that if you were miraculously to be transported, say, to Mesopotamia, you could orient yourself (at least insofar as the cardinal directions went) as soon as the sun rose or set.

Zanthodon has no sun, and its luminance never wavers or dims. Hence "east" is a handy term, nothing more.

Since first Professor Potter and I had descended in my helicopter into Zanthodon, we had made both friends and enemies. Our friends were the blond and stalwart fighting men of the Cro-Magnon nations of Sothar and Thandar. They are not only superb physical specimens, mighty warriors, fearless hunters, but also fine human beings—brave, loyal, chivalrous, and honest.

Together with a small party of these warriors, and my friend Hurok of Kor, one of the Neanderthaloid Drugars, we had entered upon these plains in pursuit of the Barbary Pirates who had carried off my beloved Princess, Darya of Thandar, when we were surprised by the Dragonmen and quickly captured.

That is to say, the Professor and I had been captured. I had commanded my warriors to scatter and disperse, and to conceal themselves, in order that the pursuit and rescue of Darya might continue even though I was no longer there to lead it.

And so we rode, mounted on the back of a gigantic reptile that stalked across the plains, great clawed three-toed feet plowing through the swishing meadow grasses, like a thing out of nightmare. Our wrists had been securely but not uncomfortably tied behind our backs, and we had been relieved of our weapons. However, we were captives, and the free of heart find captivity rankling in the extreme.

Thus I chafed, jaw set grimly, inwardly cursing my fate. As for my scrawny companion, he was afire with scientific curiosity. This was about the closest he had yet come to one of the monster saurians, and he was enjoying the experience—yes, even the musky, reptilian stench which was thick and rank in our nostrils, and the rasp of its pebbly hide against our bare thighs.

"Think of it, my boy!" he breathed ecstatically, eyes aglow with fervor behind his slightly askew pince-nez, his sun helmet wobbling on his baldish head, his tattered and travel-stained khakis mere rags by this time, through which his bony ribs and skinny arms and legs protruded comically. "These marvelous people have actually *domesticated the dinosaurs!*"

"I am thinking of it, Doc," I grunted a bit sourly. "And I'm wondering if we've been brought along to serve as fodder when the critters get peckish."

"Nonsense!" he snorted. "Reptiles of this size would regard the two of us as a mere morsel, not even a snack, and in no way to be considered luncheon."

"That's a relief," I commented.

"And a marvelous people they are, or were," he amended, studying the slender limbs and naked backs of our captor, who was seated directly in front of us. "The Minoan civilization of ancient Crete was one of the wonders of antiquity! When even the Greeks were still chasing reindeer and hitting each other in the head with rocks, the Cretans had developed their civilization to astonishing heights. Their palaces had flush toilets and hot and cold running water more than fifteen centuries before the Romans—and their cities possessed a sewage system which not even the Romans ever equaled!"

"Terrific," I snapped. "But what the hell are they doing down *here?*"

"Oh, Galloping Galileo, my boy, stop being so snippy!" he said. "Relax and enjoy the unique experience we are having, about which we can do nothing, anyway. As I—ker-*hem!* As I was saying . . . Oh, you asked a question? Yes, well, let me see . . . their island civilization was virtually destroyed at its height overnight when the volcanic island of Thera blew its top in one of the most gigantic explosions this side of Krakatoa. Knossus was shaken by the impact and partially burned; the tidal wave raised by the explosion demolished the Cretan fleet and drowned the capital. The Minoans never recovered from that devastating cataclysm, and dwindled into legend. But it would seem that a remnant fled the island and found their way here—but whether they had already left Crete before the explosion occurred, or after, remains a moot point."

"Our friend Xask seems right at home," I commented sourly, nodding toward the enigmatic little man mounted on the next dinosaur. Although his wrists, like ours, were bound behind his back, the wily and cunning former Grand Vizier of Kor maintained an unruled demeanor. His aplomb was superb acting, for the Professor and I were well aware that the Empress of Zar had long ago exiled him, banishing him from the kingdom, never to return on pain of instant execution. And here he had been captured as well . . . for, although Xask had not been one of my party of warriors, he had been stealthily following us across the plains, for mysterious motives of his own.

Catching my eye, Xask smiled a cool, thin-lipped smile. I scowled and he glanced away serenely.

From time to time, the Dragonmen conversed among themselves, their leader, whose brows were bound by a filet of odd coppery-red silver metal, giving orders and directions. Whenever this occurred, Professor Potter listened closely.

"I can almost make out what they are saying," he murmured to me. "My theories on the nature of Minoan as it was spoken are triumphantly vindicated! Very close to some of the archaic Greek dialects of Ionia, yet with a large percentage of Mesopotamian loan-words with strong Semitic roots. . . ."

I grunted; actually, I've knocked around that end of the Mediterranean long enough, mingling with Greeks, Turks, Armenians, Arabs, Copts, and the like, to have picked up more than a smattering of all their various lingoes—and, as I still retained quite a surprising amount of my college Greek, I could make out some of what they were saying myself. But then, I've always had a knack for picking up languages easily, which has saved my hide more than once.

We had been riding due east across the plains for what seemed like two hours. I was hungry, thirsty, tired, and in a dangerous mood. Spoiling for a fight. All I wanted was to get my hands free and tackle a couple of the little brown men. I was heartily sick of being captured, and the weeks or months I had spent in Zanthodon (and it had become damned hard to figure out how much time is passing when time is no longer divided into days and nights, but just consists of one endless and interminable afternoon!) had been nothing but one captivity after another.

First, the Professor and I had been captured by a band of Drugar slavers, which was bad enough. More recently, we had been taken prisoner by a weird underground race of strange, vile little men who worshiped as living gods a ghastly species of gigantic and vampiric leeches; these had designated us as offerings—walking bloodbanks, you might say, and involuntary ones, to boot. We had only just gotten free of the cavern-folk, when the Dragonmen of Zar had chanced our way.

You never miss your freedom so dearly, I have found, as when you have briefly enjoyed it, only to have it snatched away again.

In a word, I was keeping my eyes open, trying to figure out a way to escape with the Professor. As for Xask, let him save his own hide, if possible. I owed the treacherous little Machiavelli nothing—and, come to think of it, *he* had taken me prisoner once, too!

If I'd had my .45 automatic in my belt, it would have been a different story. The slugs probably wouldn't have so much as dented the hides of the dinosaurs, but they would have put the fear of Colt into the Minoans!

But the gun was long gone, curse the luck, and I'd been having a lot of bad luck recently.

Just then the leader of the party gave a brief command and the advance halted for lunch. As if in obedience to some unheard order, the monstrous reptiles came to a halt and began hooting and honking—for all the world like a herd of cows mooing to be let out of pasture.

The captain—his name seemed to be Raphad—snapped brusque commands. The dinosaurs were unharnessed, saddlebags unpacked, and fires lit in portable charcoal braziers. The delicious odors of roasting steaks caressed our nostrils.

"Look!" breathed the Professor. Far across the plains we spied a herd of huge elk-like quadrupeds. Honking hungrily, the saurians went galloping off in their direction, and about the time we were enjoying our luncheon, they were having their own. Which put my fears at rest concerning the purpose of our having been captured, anyway: whatever it might lead to, we were obviously not designed as dinner for the dinos!

Raphad saw that we were untied and permitted us to relieve ourselves—two hours of riding a galloping dinosaur can do brutal things to the human kidneys, I assure you!—then ceramic bowls of a sort of spicy vegetable mush were handed to us, complete with wooden spoons, leather jacks of a sweet red wine not unlike Mavrodaphne, and hunks of sizzling steak speared on wooden sticks like shish kebab.

We fell to hungrily, and before long I felt a lot better.

Captain Raphad himself came over. Squatting on his heels, he regarded us with not unfriendly curiosity.

"Can you understand my speech?" he inquired.

"About one word out of three," I admitted. "And please speak slowly."

He smiled understandingly, then nodded to where Xask sat alone, fastidiously devouring his own lunch. "Are you the friends of the Prince?"

"Not us," I said emphatically. "As a matter of fact, he's done us dirty more times than once, and I'd love to take a poke at him."

The captain looked blank for a moment, then laughed. "Your colloquialisms are a trifle obscure," he chuckled, "but I think I take your meaning. You were, however, in his company...."

I shook my head. "On the contrary, he was following us—I don't know why. Listen, can you tell us where you are taking us?"

He blinked. "But I thought you knew!"

"We don't. We are strangers to these parts, and have barely even heard of your people or your land."

He regarded me with a strange expression in his bright black eyes.

"You are being taken as slaves to the greatest city in all the world, there to be offered as living sacrifices to the immortal goddess," he said.

This astounding statement was made with a straight face.

I have to admit, it took my breath away.

"Well, just so long as we *know*," I said weakly.

Chapter 2

A DIFFICULT DECISION

As the herd of giant dinosaurs dwindled into the distance, the long grasses which clothed the level plain stirred, and men rose to their feet, staring after the reptiles.

For the most part, they were tall and stalwart fighting-men, dressed in little more than a scrap of hide twisted about their loins and sandals on their feet. Some were bearded and some clean-shaven; all save one were tanned, lithe, blond, with clear blue eyes and handsome faces.

One, however, although blond, had scraggly hair, mean little eyes and a skinny frame. This was the wily Murg, a cowardly little Sotharian who had accompanied us, albeit reluctantly, since there was nothing else to do.

The other man was a hulking monstrosity, compared to the smooth-skinned Cro-Magnon warriors. He stood nearly seven feet tall on his splayed feet, and his huge, sloping shoulders and long, heavily muscled, apelike arms were thatched with dirty russet fur, as was the breadth of his massive chest. He had an underslung prognathous jaw, dim little eyes buried under thick shelf-like brows of protruding bone, a painful inch of brow under the tangle of his matted hair. His body was wrapped in dirty hides; he clenched a long, stone-bladed spear, and a stone axe, heavy as a sledgehammer, dangled from thongs at his waist.

His name was Hurok.

The youngest of the Cro-Magnon warriors was a handsome boy named Jorn the Hunter, one of the tribesmen of Thandar. The youth stared after the herd of reptiles as they vanished in the distance, and his strong young jaw was grimly set as if to belie the unmanly tears that blurred his eyes.

"That we, his warriors, should stand idly by—nay, should hide in the grasses like cowardly uld!—while our chieftain, Eric Carstairs, is borne away by the Dragonmen of Zar is a disgrace to our manhood!" the boy cried, his voice shaking a little with the intensity of his emotion.

Varak of Sothar clapped the youth on the shoulder, companionably.

"I know, boy," he said. "We all feel miserable about it, not just you. But, remember, the last order which Eric Carstairs gave us before his capture was that we do just as we did."

"Aye," said another warrior, one Parthon. "And had we not, we should all have been taken prisoner—or been slain."

"Better to die defending our chieftain and our honor than to live like cowards!" spat Jorn the Hunter fiercely.

"We live," said a deep voice from behind him in somber tones. "And thus we may follow and rescue our chieftain and his friend."

Jorn turned to look Hurok of the Kor up and down. If he had not been so upset, I strongly doubt that the boy would have uttered the phrase he uttered then.

"What does a Drugar know of honor?" the youth snarled.

Hurok blinked as if he had been struck; then his face darkened and his mighty hand curled about the haft of the heavy axe which hung at his side.

"As much as any panjani," he growled. "And perhaps more—"

Varak stepped between the two, his hands raised to mollify.

"Let us not quarrel! Are we not comrades—Drugar or panjani? There is much in the words Hurok has spoken: we have saved our lives, and our freedom, by behaving like cowards, even as Jorn has said. It now remains for us to employ our lives and our freedom in a cause which will redeem our lost honor."

"It was the wish of Eric Carstairs that we pursue the men-that-ride-on-water, and rescue the Princess from their hands," murmured Ragor of Thandar. His comrade, Erdon, nodded in agreement.

Jorn's eyes faltered and fell. "That is true, I had forgotten," he whispered in a low voice, ashamed of his outburst. Ragor clapped him on the back.

"We are all distressed that our chieftain is gone, boy," he said. "It now remains for us to decide which course of action to follow. What say you all, friends—shall we follow the track of the Dragonmen and seek an opportunity to rescue our chieftain and the old man, his companion—or shall we

continue on in the path along which Eric Carstairs was leading us, to the rescue of Darya of Thandar?"

Each of the warriors eyed the other, no one wishing to
speak up first. Either course of action was equally dangerous,
and neither was certain of success.

Jorn spoke up at last.

"As for myself, I will devote my honor to the Princess,"
the boy said stoutly. For much of her recent adventures,
Darya had gone championed by Jorn, who was a youth of
her own tribe, and the lad regarded her with unselfish devotion.

Varak studied the Apeman of Kor with inquisitive eyes.
The Sotharian warrior, one of those I had rescued from hideous captivity in the cavern-city, knew that Hurok was among
the panjani only by sufferance and because of his close
friendship with Eric Carstairs.

"What is the decision of Hurok?" inquired the Sotharian.

The mighty Drugar regarded him in silence. Then he
spoke.

"Hurok will pursue the Dragonmen and give his life, if
needs he must, to help his friend," he said stolidly.

"Well spoken," nodded Varak approvingly. "But—what if
the rest of us choose to follow the Princess?"

"Then Hurok will go alone to save Black Hair from the
men of Zar."

Cringing little Murg now had gathered enough courage to
speak his mind. "Would it not be wiser far for us to return to
the main body of the host, and to apprise the High Chiefs of
Sothar and of Thandar of what had chanced to occur?" he
whined. "Then a mighty band of warriors could split, half to
pursue the stolen Princess and the other half to rescue Eric
Carstairs!"

"To do so would lose the advantage," said Hurok. "Even
now, the Dragonmen recede from us rapidly, for their beasts
can stride more swiftly than a man may run. Ere we could
return to the host, they would be very far away. The warriors
must decide now what they will do."

"Then let each man speak in turn," suggested Varak. "As
for myself, Varak of Sothar will follow the spoor of the great
beasts and attempt to rescue Eric Carstairs."

One by one, the little band spoke its mind. Murg wished to
return to the safety of the host, while Warza and Parthon
wished to aid the Princess. Ragor and Erdon were mightily
inclined to that mode of action, as well, feeling that the

cave-girl needed their help more urgently than did Eric Carstairs or the Professor, who were, after all, men, and therefore presumably—according to the manly code of this harsh,
prehistoric world—able to fend for themselves. Jorn stoutly
determined to seek the Princess.

"Very well," said Hurok. "Hurok of Kor will go his way,
then." And without further words, the hulking Neanderthal
began to truss his weapons securely to him, binding the spear
across his broad shoulders with thongs and strapping the
stone axe against his hairy thigh. It was obvious that the Apeman intended to run after the Zarian party, so as not to permit them the advantage of drawing even farther ahead.

The Cro-Magnons watched him with uncertainty in their
hearts. It was true that they yearned to rescue their chieftain;
also, it was tantamount to desertion to permit the lone Drugar to go off into the wilderness, somehow to stage a one-man
war against the feared Dragonmen. They rather felt as if they
were deserting him—and Eric Carstairs, as well.

As Hurok prepared to depart, Jorn laid one hand tentatively upon his massive arm. The Apeman peered down at
the handsome youth inquiringly.

"If Hurok permits," breathed Jorn fiercely, "Jorn of Thandar will accompany him. Two fighting men may succeed,
whereas one man, however mighty a warrior, would certainly
fail."

"It will please Hurok to have Jorn the Hunter at his side,"
said the Apeman with simple dignity.

Varak sighed. "And, surely, *three* will have a better chance
of success, than two," he said resignedly, stepping to join
them.

Hurok grunted and his lips twitched. The moody Neanderthal almost smiled, but not quite.

The others looked at each other with indecision. Finally,
Ragor, Erdon, Warza, and Parthon stepped forward to join
the party.

"When we are so very few already, it seems foolish to
divide our numbers," said Parthon philosophically.

Only Murg wavered, fear visible in his dry, twitching lips
and bulging eyes. With every fibre of his miserable little
being, the scrawny Sotharian yearned for the safety of numbers. And yet he feared to traverse the plains, the savage
jungles, the mysterious promontory, and the hills alone.

Finally, snuffling hopelessly, he shuffled after the others.

It was Hurok who set the pace. It mattered little to him whether he went after Eric Carstairs alone or in the company of the other warriors. For he had intended all along to pursue the Dragonmen and to do whatever could be done to rescue the first panjani who had ever treated him like a friend and an equal.

The splay-footed Neanderthal was not exactly built for running. Hurok must have tipped the scales at three hundred pounds, and the best runners are lightly and trimly built—Jorn, for instance. But Hurok had strength and iron endurance and enough grim, single-minded determination to make three other men. And the pace he set, while a grueling one, was not beyond the powers of any of his comrades, save possibly Murg, who very soon fell behind, whining and snuffling and complaining.

"Varak could wish that Murg had chosen *not* to accompany us," admitted Varak to Hurok who trotted along at his side.

The Neanderthal grunted noncommittally.

"Surely, he will only slow us down, and when it comes to fighting, and it will certainly come to that in the end, you know," chatted Varak, who was a bit loquacious and of a humorous, mischievous bent of mind, "when it comes to fighting, he will be even more of a hindrance than a help. What is the opinion of Hurok?"

The huge Drugar grunted sourly and spat.

"It is the opinion of Hurok," he said, "that Varak would be wise to save his breath for running, not waste it in talk."

And with that, he drew ahead of the Sotharian warrior and forged on in the front.

"Um," said Varak lamely, wincing. Then he stopped talking and saved his breath for running, as he had been advised.

Chapter 3

THE MYSTERY OF THE CIRCLET

As we ate, I pondered gloomily our chances of making an escape. If we were to attempt it, now would seem to be the time, for we were both untied, although our ankles were tethered, and the Dragonmen would be hampered in their attempts to pursue us as it would take them some time to round up their reptiles again.

I said as much to the Professor. Chewing on his steak, he gave me a dubious look.

"But they are all around us, my boy, and are a dozen or more to our two," he observed.

"Yeah, but I bet—with a bit of a head start—we could outrun them," I said. This was probably true, certainly of myself, and of the Professor as well. I had seen the old scientist in a sprint before, and, while he is not exactly Olympic material, those skinny legs were capable of a very decent pace, given strong enough motives for flight.

"And if we do not outrun them, what next?" he inquired. "We have nothing but our bare hands with which to fight, while they are armed. . . ."

Of course, that was so. The little olive-skinned Minoans bore short bronze blades which rather resembled the ancient Roman *gladius*, and other weapons as well: poniard-like long daggers, slender spears of some glittering, unfamiliar metal, lassos, and three weighted balls on a cord. This last implement bore a strong similarity to the bolo of the Argentine gauchos, and was probably used in the same way.

I balled one fist and let him look at it.

"Bare hands can be decent weapons, you know," I said suggestively.

"Um," he remarked doubtfully. "It does seem to me unlikely that we could elude recapture for very long . . . out on this interminable plain, there is simply nowhere to go and, quite certainly, nowhere to hide. Once they have remounted, they have only to ride us down and seize us again."

I knew that he was right, of course, but it irked me to be taken captive again, after winning my freedom so very recently. I said as much to the older man, with a surly tone.

"I feel much the same way, Eric," he agreed. "But would it not be wiser to wait until an even better opportunity presents itself? To try to escape now, and to fail in the attempt, would only put the Zarians on their guard. They would watch us from that point on with redoubled vigilance, and our chances for another try at getting away would be few and frail. . . ."

"Watch it, here comes Xask," I growled. The Minoan renegade, finishing his lunch and wiping his lips fastidiously on a bit of fabric, now rose to his feet and sauntered over to where we sat, with a pleasant smile on his smooth face.

"Well, Eric Carstairs," he said mildly, "the fortunes of war seem to have turned the tables once again. Formerly, you were *my* captive—my deeply honored guest, rather—and here we are, both the, ah, 'guests' of my fellow countrymen."

He didn't exactly use the above colloquialisms, but you get the idea. I said nothing, giving him a contemptuous glance, then ignoring him. The Professor, however, had the gall to engage the fellow in conversation.

"Tell me, Xask, why did you—as it were—volunteer for capture by the soldiers?" he demanded. The other smiled.

"Since I was unfortunate enough to lose the friendship of the Sacred Empress and to earn sufficient enmity as to be driven into outlawry, I have not exactly enjoyed my exile. For a while, as you know, I found a safe haven of refuge among the Apemen of Kor, and rose to a position of influence with the late Uruk, the then High Chief. But life, among the bestial Drugars, for a man of my sophistication, was far from pleasant. I have yearned for a method whereby I might regain the favor of the Empress . . . and thanks to you, Eric Carstairs, I believe that I have found it."

"Oh, yeah?" I said skeptically. "And what's the trick you have up your sleeve this time?"

With a bland smile, he opened a flap in his tunic. To my amazement I glimpsed the blue steel barrel of my long-lost automatic! He had taken it from me when One-Eye jumped me earlier, but I had assumed he would have thrown it aside in his panicky flight when he ran from the charging aurochs.

I did not at this time know that Xask had already used the gun at least once, and had a canny notion of its powers. Now a dreadful foreboding entered my heart, however, curiously combined with a lifting of my hopes. For if I could get the automatic from Xask, the Professor and I would have a mighty good chance of getting free of the Minoans.

He was watching the expression in my eyes, and easily withdrew a bit from close proximity to me, concealing the pistol beneath his garments once again.

"I have observed your marvelous thunder-weapon in action, Eric Carstairs," he drawled lazily. And by that I guessed that he had been watching from the underbrush at the edge of the jungle when I had put a bullet through Uruk's brain during the battle between the warriors of Thandar and the Apemen of Kor.

"So?"

"So . . . if you will only teach me the secrets of its manufacture, I'll have a potent weapon to present to the Empress upon my return to the Scarlet City," he said smoothly. "Armed with a number of thunder-weapons of similar design and composition, the legions of Zar can easily conquer all of Zanthodon. For no comparable force exists to delay their march to victory, as they will be opposed by mere bands of savages armed with spears and stone axes!"

The audacity of his plan was stunning. Also, it turned my stomach: I could visualize the brave and gallant warriors of Sothar or Thandar charging the legions of Zar and being cut to ribbons by bullets from guns patterned after mine. The picture was sickening.

"I will not cooperate, surely you know that," I told him levelly.

He shrugged good-humoredly.

"We none of us can know what we are capable of doing if the proper inducements are employed," he pointed out with a twinkle of cold menace in his eye.

I didn't care for the sound of that, for he was right, of course. Once, he had threatened to have One-Eye work me over unless I told him the secrets of the .45, and the only thing that saved me that time had been the aurochs charging us.

I tried to look grimly determined, but just then, Raphad came over to rebind our wrists, as it was time to mount up and ride on, and we had no more time to pursue this conversation.

In obedience to some unheard signal, the herd of dinosaurs left their feasting and came stalking back across the plain to be resaddled by their masters. The sight fascinated Professor Potter and piqued his curiosity.

"Tell me, Captain, by what means do you control the great beasts?" he inquired. "I certainly heard no whistle or other call summoning them, and from what I know of their kind, the dragons are simply too stupid to be easily domesticated and too unruly to be kept for very long in a state of docility."

Raphad touched the circlet which adorned his brows. I have mentioned it before, but as he was the only man in the troop who wore one, I had assumed it to be a mark of his military rank. Now, looking more closely at it, I noticed that the band of peculiar ruddy silver was set with a large faceted stone like a clear crystal.

"By means of this," he replied enigmatically. Then he turned away to oversee the remounting of his troops. And shortly we rode on across the plain in the direction of tall mountains which loomed mistily in the distance.

Later we again dismounted and were told to rest. Our hands and ankles were freed, but leather collars were affixed about our throats, fastened by long tethers to a peg driven into the ground near where the sentries squatted keeping guard. Warm woolen blankets were taken from the dinosaurs' saddlebags and a couple were tossed over to us.

I have previously remarked in these memoirs that in a world where the daylight never dims and darkness never falls, the people become accustomed to sleeping whenever the need overtakes them. The men of Zanthodon have invented no way of measuring the passage of time—indeed, they have hardly any concept of time at all, for to them there is nothing but an eternal Now. This being so, they do not divide time into equal intervals of waking or sleeping, but simply sack out any time they feel like it.

The only exception I have ever found to this custom is the way the people of the caverns separated time into "wakes" and "sleeps." But their life was heavily regimented by the late, unlamented Gorpaks, who presumably liked things neat and orderly.

Like myself, the Professor had a hard time getting to sleep. For although we were weary from hours in the saddle, captivity among a mysterious new race had us too tense and keyed up to find repose in slumber. For one thing, the Professor was still puzzling his wits over the enigma of the circlet Raphad wore.

"Did you notice the odd hue of the metal?" he inquired. "Reddish, yet silvery . . . an alloy of copper with silver? But for what reason? Both substances, of course, are excellent conductors of electrical impulses . . . but what purpose does the crystal serve, do you suppose?"

"Beats me," I muttered. "Let's get some shut-eye."

"Some forms of crystal are capable of storing electrical charges, of course," he said ruminatively, oblivious to my remark. "The galena crystals, for example, used in the old-time crystal radio sets. . . ."

"Let's solve the secrets of nature later on, okay, Doc? I'm getting sleepy just listening to you."

"Something about the faceting of the crystal, though, reminds me of a lens or a prism," he rambled on. "I say, Eric, do you suppose the metal band conducts the electrical impulses of thought in the mind of the wearer, which is then focused into a beam of narrow intensity by the lens-like crystal, permitting the Zarians to dominate the giant reptiles by *telepathy?*"

"Could be," I mumbled, drifting off.

"Remarkable!" he breathed. "Eternal Einstein, what a feat! The Minoans have ascended the scale of civilization during the millennia they have dwelt here in Zanthodon, achieving astounding heights. To discover the conductive properties of the two metals silver and copper—to create the alloy alone—"

Suddenly he stopped, thunder-struck.

He reached over and shook my shoulder, rousing me from my doze.

"Mmph?" I inquired drowsily.

"The reddish silver, my boy! The very hue Plato ascribed to the mystery-metal *orichalcum* in his dialogues, *Critias* and *Timaeus!* Do you realize what this means?"

"Mmph?"

"*Orichalcum* was the metal of Atlantis!" he cried, marveling. "The theories of certain authorities must be accurate, after all. Eric, my boy . . . *we have been captured by the last surviving descendants of the ancient Atlanteans!*"

"Tell me all about it in the mornin'," I suggested, rolling over.

Chapter 4

HUROK MAKES A FRIEND

Even though they didn't want to, Hurok and his companions had to pause to rest and eat something. Jorn surprised a nesting uld in the long grasses, and brought the plump beast down with an arrow from his bow. Varak made fire in the time-honored way of the Stone Age, by striking two flints together. In time the sparks ignited in a heap of dry grass, and more quickly than it would take me to describe, Uld cutlets were roasting over a merry blaze.

There was no source of fresh water to be discovered in their immediate vicinity, but some of the warriors had leather bottles like army canteens suspended from their waists by thongs, and these were passed around so that the weary Cro-Magnons could refresh their thirst.

Hurok squatted on his heels a little distance from the others. The Drugar felt distinctly out of place and rather uncomfortable in the company of the panjani. Of all the smooth-skinned kind, it was only Eric Carstairs (whom he thought of as "Black Hair") with whom he had found acceptance and true comradeship. He said, therefore, as little as possible to the others, responding only to direct questions, and otherwise maintained a taciturn silence.

As for the warriors, it was true that they felt as uncomfortable with him as he with them. They did not even feel all that easy among themselves, for they were men from two different tribes, Thandar and Sothar. And life in the primitive world of Zanthodon is hard and cruel: since any chance-met stranger is a rival, a competitor, he was thought also to be an enemy.

Now the men of Sothar and Thandar had met while in captivity to the cavern-people, the Gorpaks. They had perforce slept together, ate together, toiled together under the lash of their evil little bandy-legged masters. Tolerance of

32

strangers they had learned because they must, but from their shared experiences the men of the two Cro-Magnon tribes had learned to trust, to rely upon, and to get along with men from the other tribe.

This did not mean they were all that easy together, it must be admitted. Xenophobia is a disease sadly common to the human animal in general, and so is prejudice. The feelings of dislike, distrust, and suspicion can be eradicated with time and patience and education. But it does not come quickly or easily.

But, while certain bonds of mutual respect had grown between the warriors of the two tribes, the situation with Hurok was quite different. From the cradle, the Cro-Magnons had learned to fear and despise the brutal, beastlike Neanderthals. Warfare had blazed continuously between Cro-Magnon and Neanderthal, and each side had very good reasons for hating the other—the memory of Cro-Magnon brothers, sisters, and friends carried off by Neanderthal slave raiders, or slaughtered in open battle, or felled from ambush by the hairy Drugars.

While Eric Carstairs had been among them, they had tolerated the presence of Hurok and grudgingly come to respect his strength and valor, his battle skills, and his devotion to their chieftain.

But now, lacking my presence to keep them in line and to smooth the difference between them, they half-guiltily resented their forced comradeship with the hulking Drugar, as he resented it for his part. There was nothing overtly hostile about these feelings, for the warriors were savages, it is true, but gentlemen of a sort. And Hurok, after all, was the friend and companion of Eric Carstairs.

But it was there, nonetheless.

After a brief respite, the warriors again took up their pursuit of the Dragon-riders, resuming their long marathon run across the plains. While they could no longer track the Dragonmen by visual means alone, since the more swifly moving Zarian party had long since gone out of sight, the enormous clawed feet of the monster lizards they rode left marks easy to discern in the grasses which clothed the plain. Following this spoor was but as child's play to men trained from the cradle to hunt and track.

They began to weary again in time, and it irked them that Hurok's powers of endurance were distinctly superior to their own, and that the Apeman paused to rest only when his companions insisted. Were it left up to Hurok, he would have run until he became completely exhausted; then, and only then, would he have paused to rest.

While his physical prowess annoyed them, it was also cause for new respect. The warriors of the Cro-Magnon prize and admire many qualities—loyalty, wisdom, judgment, courage, and skill. But the highest degree of admiration they reserve for physical strength and endurance alone.

Life in this savage, untamed wilderness is one unending battle against the ferocity of beasts and the cunning and enmity of other men. And the secret of survival against such odds is often brute strength.

And that Hurok of Kor certainly possessed.

They knew it, and it irked them. On the other hand, they could not help admiring him for it, however reluctantly.

Quite suddenly, the Cro-Magnons saw that prowess demonstrated in the most dramatic of terms.

The ground cracked open beneath their feet unexpectedly, and a head the size of a small barrel burst into view. One glimpse of that scaly snout, that fanged and gaping jaw, those cold and soulless eyes, and the warriors identified this adversary.

"A xunth!" cried Varak. "Scatter quickly!"

The warriors instantly veered off in all directions from the common center, so as to present as confusing a variety of victims as was possible. Now, the xunth, which apparently hollows out its lair beneath the earth of the plains, is a monstrously huge prehistoric serpent. At the time, I had never seen one, but I understood they could reach the astounding length of thirty feet. And thirty feet of snake is a whole lot of snake, let me assure you!

Jorn the Hunter, agile though he was, did not quite move as quickly as he should have. And when the toe of his sandal lodged in a knot of grasses, the boy took a tumble and lay prone, momentarily stunned by the fall, which had knocked the breath out of him. So when the xunth came gliding up out of his hidey-hole, there was as tempting a morsel as a xunth could ask for, virtually laid out and waiting.

Voicing a thunderous hiss, the enormous serpent lunged at the dazed youth, fanged jaws gaping wide. From a safe distance, Ragor and Erdon and Warza, who were Jorn's fellow tribesmen, cried out in alarm and came sprinting to the rescue of their young friend.

But Hurok was there first.

The Apeman of Kor had not been able to run as far as the others, for his lumbering strides were heavier and more clumsy than were theirs. Hence, when he turned and realized Jorn's deadly peril, Hurok reacted with instinctive alacrity. Whipping out his stone-bladed javelin, he cast it with all the strength of his mighty arms at the xunth.

Tough indeed was the scaly hide of the giant serpent, but strong were the arms of Hurok and unerring his aim. The keen point of the spear bit deep, sinking into the muscle of the serpent's neck, lodging directly behind the base of the skull.

Screaming in a frenzy of rage and pain, the xunth forgot all about the dazed boy sprawled helpless at its feet, and turned, attempting to snap at the thing stuck in its neck, which hurt abominably. Of course, as the snake turned its head, so also did its neck turn, and the spear shaft swung out of reach.

This gave Hurok time to unlimber his stone axe.

Springing forward, the Drugar planted both feet to either side of the fallen boy, sheltering the youth with his body. Then, as the xunth espied him and struck at this new adversary, Hurok swung the heavy axe with every ounce of the strength in his mighty arms.

He literally smashed the xunth's skull like an eggshell. Blood and brains squirmed in all directions. The serpent fell to the earth, writhing in slow death spasms. Hurok seized up Jorn and tossed him across one burly shoulder and hastily beat a retreat.

Having reached a safe distance, he let the boy down and squatted on his hunkers with the others as they watched the slow spasms which contorted the fantastic length of the dying serpent monster.

The Cro-Magnons regarded Hurok with an emotion which verged upon awe. The strength of that blow had been prodigious, was almost beyond their imagining. And the selfless courage of the Drugar, at springing to the instant defense of one who was not, after all, of his own tribe nor even of his own kind, aroused within their breasts a degree of respect they had not previously entertained toward the Apeman.

Recovering his breath, Jorn thanked Hurok for his life with simple but heartfelt words. The Apeman merely nodded, saying nothing. To such as Hurok it had been an instinct to come to the defense of a comrade, nothing more. And certainly nothing which required elaborate thanks.

Shortly thereafter, he went forward and retrieved his spear from the body of the reptile.

Having rested, however briefly, and refreshed themselves thereby, the party continued on across the plains in the direction of the distant mountains.

This time, however, a change might have been discerned in the manner in which the Cro-Magnons regarded their hulking and ugly companion. They no longer avoided meeting his eyes or excluded him from the general conversation, although Hurok was, as always, glum and taciturn, despising casual speech.

But he was no longer quite as much an outsider among them as he had been.

Later, when the need for sleep overcame them and they were forced to make camp, they sat together around the fire, sharing their small stores of food and drink equally; no longer did Hurok of Kor sit apart from them.

And when they sought sleeping places amid the meadow grasses, Jorn deliberately chose a nest very near to the place which Hurok had taken for himself.

If the Apeman noticed, he made no comment. At length, Jorn spoke up a shade timidly.

"Good sleeping, O Hurok," the boy said.

"Good sleeping to you, Jorn," grunted Hurok emotionlessly.

You never know exactly how or when you are going to make a good friend. But friends come in handy, especially in a world like Zanthodon.

And Hurok had made a friend.

Chapter 5

THE MARCH OF
THE WARRIORS

While these events were taking place on the plains to the north of the jungle-clad promontory, yet other things were happening at the scene of our earlier adventures.

Tharn of Thandar, the magnificent jungle monarch, had by now returned from the cavern-city with all of his warriors, scouts, and huntsmen. The scouring of the cavern-city was complete, and the last of the Gorpaks had been slain; as well, the victorious Cro-Magnons had thoroughly eradicated the hideous, vampiric Sluagghs.

The pale, languid cavern-folk, now released from their long slavery, tasted freedom for the first time in their lives. One assumes they heartily enjoyed the flavor of it, although the taste was a new one for them.

Returning from the caverns, with Garth and his Sotharians at his side, Tharn learned from those of the women and the wounded who had remained in the clearing that his daughter, Darya, had been stolen away with the Professor. When he heard that it was the villainous traitor, Fumio, together with Xask, who had done this deed, the brows of Tharn darkened thunderously.

"We shall enter the jungles at once to pursue the traitor," he said, his deep voice stern and hard. "They cannot have gone very far."

"Eric Carstairs is already on their trail, my Omad," said one of the wounded. "With him were the Sotharian warriors of his squad, including Varak, and some of our guards, Ragor and Erdon."

"Perhaps Eric Carstairs has already caught up with the men who have thieved away the Princess Darya," said Garth,

High Chief of the warriors of Sothar. "In which case, my friend, your vengeance has already been consummated."

"We shall see," said Tharn briefly. Then, after commanding his warriors to make ready for the pursuit in full force, bringing with them the wounded as well, he turned to his brother chief.

"Will Garth, my friend, accompany us or remain here?"

"Henceforward," said Garth simply, "the warriors of Sothar will fight at the side of the warriors of Thandar. We, too, shall march to recover our friends. For, during our captivity to the vile little Gorpaks, I came to admire the courage and patience of the gomad Darya. Had I another daughter, I could wish her to be like your daughter in all ways."

The stern visage of the jungle monarch relaxed slightly, and he permitted a smile to lighten the grim set of his lips.

Without further ado the two tribes began preparations for a full-scale departure. Before Zanthodon was an hour older, they had vanished into the jungles.

The scouts and huntsmen of the two tribes were arranged in a wide semicircle, so as to comb the brush in advance of the main body of the warriors. Their keen eyes missed little as they glided noiselessly through the trees and bushes, searching for the slightest clue as to the whereabouts of the missing Princess and her abductors.

Erelong they found the dead body of One-Eye in a small clearing. The ungainly corpse was sprawled in a pool of congealing blood, mouth open, glazed eyes staring sightlessly. Tharn regarded the cadaver with puzzlement: he could not recall having ever seen this Drugar, and as the war party from Kor was believed to have perished to the last warrior in the stampede of the thantors, it baffled him that a Drugar should be in these parts, far from the place where the rest of his kind had been trampled by the lumbering pachyderms.

One of the Thandarian scouts knelt to examine the corpse. He rose, his expression puzzled.

"My Omad, the Drugar has been slain in a most peculiar manner, by an edged weapon of strong metal, such as I can scarcely imagine," the scout reported.

This only increased the mystery. Perhaps I should explain at this point, that the Cro-Magnons employ knives, axes, spears, and bows; they have never invented the sword and neither have their old adversaries, the Apemen of Kor. If I had been on the scene, I could, of course, have told Tharn that it had been the Barbary Pirates—the Men-That-Ride-Upon-The-Water—who had struck One-Eye down. But Tharn knew nothing of the Barbary Pirates, or very little, having never seen them in action or observed their weapons.

"We have naught else to learn here," he said, "so let us continue on."

Beyond the jungles, which they traversed without any further discoveries, the Stone Age warriors came eventually to the beach. And there they found and recognized the tracks in the sand which had been made by my comrades and myself when we had gone around the peninsula, hoping to pursue the Pirates.

As the sandals of the Thandarians and the men of Sothar used different stitching, it was not difficult for the scouts to guess that these were the tracks of myself and my party. It was equally obvious that we had been pursuing those who had carried off Darya.

The two tribes followed our trail around the promontory and at length discovered the great northern plain. By this time, of course, Hurok and the others were far off across the immensity of the plain, and not even the eagle-like gaze of the Cro-Magnon scouts could have glimpsed them in the distance. But here, of course, the trail ended, for the long grasses wherewith the plain was thickly grown do not hold the footprints of men, and to have found some sign or token of our passage would have been extremely difficult.

Arms folded upon his mighty chest, Tharn stared broodingly out into the distance. He knew that Eric Carstairs and a party of Thandarian and Sotharian warriors were in close pursuit of his daughter, but nowhere on the plain could he see aught of our whereabouts. In which direction, therefore, should he continue the march? Tharn conferred briefly with his chieftains and with his fellow Omad, Garth, eliciting their suggestions.

"It would seem wisest to Garth," said that personage, "that we continue along the shores of the Sogar-Jad. Somewhere farther in that direction, we may yet catch up with the abductors or with their pursuers, or discover some further sign to guide us."

This seemed advisable to the mind of Tharn, as well; there was, of course, no reason for him to think of striking out into the center of the plain, which was actually the direction in which we had gone, hoping to find a shortcut. At this region the shoreline bulged outwards, curving back upon itself far-

ther to the north. We had taken the most direct route,
straight across the plain, to save time. But this did not occur
to the Cro-Magnons.

They marched north along the coast of the prehistoric
ocean, with no idea of where they were going or of what they
might find when they got there.

For some reason, a large number of men do not seem to
be able to advance with the speed a single man, or a small
party, can attain. And, in the case of the Cro-Magnon tribesmen, they were slowed in their progress by the necessity of
favoring those of their number who had been wounded in the
battle which freed the cavern-folk from the Gorpaks. As well,
a number of the women of Sothar were with them, including
Nian, the mate of Garth, and her daughter, Yualla, a lithe,
handsome girl who was about the same age as Jorn the
Hunter.

I say this with some reservations, for, in a world without
day or night, a world without seasons, whose inhabitants have
not the least conception of the passage of time, it is uniquely
difficult to judge the age of anyone.

As they marched along the coast, the hunters of the two
tribes, ranging far, found and slew a number of plump uld,
and their skillful archers brought down several zomak, an ancestor of the birds of the Upper World which Professor Potter considers to be the archaeopteryx. They are odd-looking
and ungainly fowl—imagine a bird with teeth, who has as
many scales as he has feathers—but not at all bad tasting. Especially if you happen to be hungry.

And by this time, the tribes had developed quite an appetite. Finding themselves on the edge of a small stream of
fresh water which meandered across the plain to mingle with
the waves of the Sogar-Jad, they made camp. While the
women built fires and prepared to cook the game taken by
the huntsmen, the men drank, bathed, and rested. While
speed was uppermost in the mind of Tharn, a wise chief
knows that men must rest from time to time, in order that
they may maintain a steady pace. So, while it gnawed at him
that they must loiter here, wasting time and yielding yet further advantage to the abductors of his daughter, loiter they
must and did, but briefly.

It is not my intention to narrate the march of the tribesmen in any great detail, not only because nothing in particu-

lar happened of interest along the trail, but also because I have more significant events to relate. Suffice it to say that after several wakes and sleeps, the Thandarians and Sotharians reached the point at which the shoreline curves back upon itself, and found the northernmost extremity of the continent.

Here a broad arm of the underground sea extended like a natural barrier, making further progress impossible. Along this arm of the Sogar-Jad were many small and rocky islands—a veritable archipelago, in fact. They were the roosting places of sea fowl, as could be ascertained by the white droppings with which they were littered.

But beyond these small islands along the shore, and in the very midst of the sea, was a large island of naked rock. And it was there that Tharn of Thandar and his men saw a sight such as few of them had ever seen or even imagined.

It was a ship of the Barbary Pirates.

With its high, pointed prow and immense spread of canvas, the green banner of Islam fluttering from its height, the vessel was a sight which astounded the cavemen. It would, in fact, have astounded you or me, for such a ship has not sailed the seas of the Upper World within the memory of any living man; only in historical paintings could you have seen such a vessel as now met the gaze of Tharn of Thandar and his companions.

"It is the Men-That-Ride-Upon-The-Water," he said wonderingly. All about him, the warriors and scouts and huntsmen stood and stared as the magnificent vessel sailed by, dwindling into the misty distance.

"Let us continue along the way," he said after the ship had vanished from sight.

Had he but known that the mysterious vessel was none other than the pirate galley commanded by Kâiradine Barbarossa, called Redbeard, bound for the island fortress of the corsairs, El-Cazar, with his daughter and Fumio aboard as helpless captives, I have no doubt that Tharn of Thandar would have given very different orders. . . .

Part Two

Part Two

THE
SCARLET
CITY

Chapter 6

THE GATES OF ZAR

More waking and sleeping periods passed than I can recall before the Dragonmen reached the distant range of mountains. They were tall and rugged, these mountains, and their upper reaches were used by the fearsome thakdols, or pterodactyls, for nesting purposes. This we could tell from the fact that our approach disturbed the flying lizards.

Raphad assured us, however, that we were in no danger from the winged monstrosities. The captain seemed not unfriendly, and, in fact, entertained a lively curiosity concerning us. And I think he was anticipating some sort of a dramatic confrontation between the exiled Xask and this mysterious Goddess-Empress of which we had heard so much. Raphad doubtless looked forward to a good show when the Queen of Zar came face-to-face with the man she had driven into outlawry.

Despite Raphad's assurances, I kept a wary eye aloft. The monster pterodactyls of Zanthodon are more to be feared than many of the lumbering dinosaurs, most of whom, after all, are harmless vegetarians. The thakdols, on the contrary, are mindless engines of mad ferocity, and will attack a grown man on whim.

The Professor, noticing my apprehensive glances aloft, spoke up reassuringly.

"What the good captain probably alludes to, Eric my boy, is the crystal-studded circlet he wears. After all, if the power of the orichalcum filet can control these enormous monsters we are riding, it can doubtless fend off the pterodactyls."

I saw his point, but I still felt uneasy. However, we were not attacked, so perhaps the Professor was right.

The Minoans led us into a narrow pass the mouth of which wound through the range of mountains. From both sides of the mouth of this pass, gigantic stone masks glared down upon us. They had been cunningly hewn out of the stone

45

cliffs and represented horrible reptilian monsters with fanged jaws agape, as if grinning in anticipation of a coming meal.

The appearance of those ominous stone heads did nothing to calm my trepidations, either.

Xask nodded at them. "These are the Gates of Zar, Eric Carstairs," he explained. "Beyond this point, no man of Zanthodon may venture uninvited, on peril of his life. Zar needs no other barrier than the fear its name excites among the savages. . . ."

"Terrific," I said sarcastically. "What kind of creature do the stone heads represent, anyway?"

He shot me a glance of chill amusement, with just a touch of malice in it.

"They are likenesses of the God." He smiled. "And rather true to life, I fancy."

We rode on into the pass between the mountains.

I was cudgeling my wits, striving to recall what bits and pieces of information I could remember about ancient Crete. I had been on the island once, but not long enough for any sight-seeing. I remembered some odds and ends of the old Greek myths about Theseus and the Minotaur and King Minos and boys and girls dancing naked with bulls, but that was about it. I have no doubt but that the Professor could have talked for a couple of hours straight on the subject, but felt disinclined to invite a lecture. Besides, Captain Raphad, who had been treating us decently thus far, didn't much like our talking together. I suppose he feared we were plotting an escape, and if we got away from him, for all I knew, it might cost the little fellow his head.

When at length we emerged from the farther end of the pass, an astonishing vista greeted our eyes.

The mountains formed an immense ring. Cupped within their embrace lay a deep, bowl-shaped depression, like a great valley. But the valley was filled with water!

"Pnom-Jad," said Xask as we stared down at the expanse of waters. "The Little Sea."

I have no idea how wide it was, for the air was misty and distances can be tricky in the steady, unwavering light of the luminous skies of Zanthodon, but it looked big enough to measure up to the one of the Great Lakes. And that's quite a lot of water.

The inland sea was dotted with boats of every size and description. There were tiny fishing smacks and huge galleys with rows of oars and ornately curling prows. The Professor identified these last as warships and declared that they resembled in every particular the warships of ancient Crete.

Their sails were of saffron yellow or crimson, with huge emblems painted on them, mostly nautical motifs like stylized octopi. Huge staring eyes were painted on the prows of the ships, small and large as well, which was a Phoenician custom, I remembered. But then, for all I know, the Phoenicians were second cousins to the Minoans.

In the exact center of the inland sea was a great island. It was nothing but one vast metropolis, that island, right down to the shores. Huge squarish monolithic buildings of stone crowned the isle, and most of them were covered with smooth stucco or something like stucco, painted pink and yellow, orange and maroon, but more often than not—scarlet. In the haze of distance, the colors blended and merged into one malestrom of differing shades of red.

It was quite a sight. . . .

"The Scarlet City of Zar!" breathed Professor Potter, his watery blue eyes agleam with scientific curiosity. "What a magnificent spectacle—and how fortunate we are to be here to observe it! My boy, mighty Knossus must have looked very much like that, in the days before its destruction . . . and look at the Acropolis or Bursa!"

He indicated a group of buildings toward the center of the huge city, where the land rose to a height. A superb palace-complex crowned the height, blooming with green gardens, towering above the rest of the city.

"The residence of the Sacred Empress," Xask informed us coolly. "And also of the God . . ."

We descended into the vast, bowl-shaped depression by means of a stone-paved road which extended from the base of the cliff to the edge of the water. We rode past farms and cultivated acreage. Harvesters were at work in the fields of golden grain and others were toiling in the fragrant groves of fruit trees and in the green vineyards. Without exception, they were Cro-Magnon slaves. The only Zarians I saw were a few slender overseers, who generally reclined beneath striped awnings sipping from silver goblets.

"I gather that Zar's economy is based upon slave labor," the Professor mused, glancing alertly around him. "That may suggest that the ruling class or aristocracy is dwindling in numbers. . . ."

"That is so," said Xask agreeably. Due to the narrowness

of the road, we were riding side by side with him at this point, with Captain Raphad up ahead, unable to overhear our conversation. "The number of our births is far less than the number of deaths."

As we approached the edges of the sea, we observed a magnificent stone bridge which arched the expanse of the waters, its length supported on massive stone piers sunk in the lake bottom.

"A remarkable feat of engineering," Professor Potter breathed. "Even the ancient Minoans, I doubt, could have erected such a span. Only the Romans, a dozen centuries later. . . ."

At the entrance to the bridge we were made to dismount and the lizards we had been riding were led away to pens or corrals built along the side of the sea. I can understand that reptiles of their size might have had trouble negotiating the crowded streets of the island-city.

We crossed the bridge on foot, guards going before and behind us. With every step we took the cityscape expanded ahead of us, coming into greater clarity. It was truly immense, and incredibly old, and resembled no other city I have ever seen, except in pictures. Ornamental friezes in low relief ran around the upper stories, and here too a marine influence could be seen in the decorations, rows of identical seashells or leaping dolphins and that sort of thing. Ancient Crete had been a maritime civilization, I remembered, which probably accounted for the choice of decoration.

The streets were narrow and cobbled, filled with bustling throngs. We saw surprisingly few of the olive-skinned folk, but very many brawny, blond, blue-eyed Cro-Magnon slaves. They bore veiled women in tasseled palanquins and silk-robed men in something like sedan chairs, or worked at construction jobs, or were trotting about with bags and bales and amphorae.

We passed a market square redolent of fresh fish, olive oil, honey cakes, garlic, raw onions, cooking meat. Fat men with elaborately curled and perfumed hair, wearing altogether too many rings on their fingers, loudly hawked their wares or reclined at their ease sipping beverages and nibbling sweetmeats. Booths and stalls offered a glittering assortment of brass and copper rings, bracelets, brooches, uncut gemstones, tools, scrolls, weapons, piles of bright-colored bales of cloth, rolled carpets, odd-looking wooden furniture.

"Fascinating!" breathed the Professor, his sharp eyes missing absolutely nothing. I could well imagine how his fingers itched to be scribbling notes in the little blank-paged book he still carried with him in the rags of his khakis.

I was pretty impressed myself. Who would ever have dreamed this primitive and savage world had anything like this to surprise us with!

But Zanthodon was full of surprises, as I had already discovered, and not all of them are pleasant.

Raphad checked us in to some sort of depot for recently captured prisoners, waved one hand in a friendly good-bye, and stalked off about his business, herding his men before him. A bald and grouchy-looking clerk snapped questions at us which Xask had to answer, as we found it difficult understanding all he asked.

Then we were, all three, locked into low-roofed wicker cages and left to our own devices. At least, they untied our hands and removed the hobbles from our legs. There wasn't much room in the cramped little pens to move about, but we made ourselves as comfortable as was possible under the circumstances, chafing our limbs to get the circulation back and stretching out as best we could.

It occurred to me that here was my opportunity to grab my automatic away from Xask. But bright-eyed guards stood about watching us alertly, and this did not seem to be quite the right time for that.

His eyes on me as if he could read my every passing thought, Xask smiled a bit mockingly.

They gave us food and water.

I dozed off for a while. When I awoke, an elaborately gowned and coiffured individual stood before the cages, rapping on them with an ivory baton to wake us up.

He turned to address the guards.

"The Goddess will see the animals now," he said loftily. And I felt a qualm in the pit of my stomach.

Chapter 7

HUROK ASSUMES COMMAND

The long trek across the northern plains seemed interminable, for my friends were horribly aware that with each passing moment I might be maimed or slaughtered by the mystery men who had captured me and the Professor. But, at least, the warriors encountered no further peril on the same order of magnitude as the monstrous xunth.

They maintained the best pace of which their bodies were capable, but even men as lithe and athletic as they must pause to rest, to eat, to slumber.

When they were hungry, they broke and scattered to hunt the many small edible beasts of the plain, which they sometimes cooked and ate, and other times devoured raw, reluctant to loiter when I might be in imminent danger.

And when they were weary beyond even the limits of their endurance, they slept. With the passing of each period of wake and sleep, the unity between the Cro-Magnons and the Drugar of Kor, begun so tentatively, for a time so fragile, grew and strengthened. It was not an easy thing for simple primitives such as they to overcome the barriers of prejudice and hatred that had existed between their two kinds from time immemorial. But they tried.

Already, many factors were at work building the bonds of comradeship between them. From the very beginning, they could not but admire the enormous stamina of Hurok, his iron strength, his utter fearlessness, his indomitable battle skills, and his enduring and faithful loyalty to his friend, Black Hair. These were qualities which the men of Thandar and Sothar knew and valued, because they possessed them themselves.

It was sheer chance that had, however, provided them with

50

a higher motive for something resembling friendship toward the Apeman of Kor. And that was, of course, his unhesitating and unthinking heroism in springing to the defense of one of their number with whom he had already been in enmity. His coming to the aid of Jorn the Hunter seemed to them remarkable in the extreme, for the savage tribes of Zanthodon know only the ethics of the Bronze Age, which deem loyalty deserved only by a brother tribesman, and which consider all other strangers potential, if not actual, foes.

As well, there was yet another factor which helped to knit these diverse individuals together into a band of comrades, and that one, alas, is a trifle more difficult for me to describe, for we are speaking of the simpler children of remoter ages who have never tasted the enervating luxuries and conveniences of modern urban civilization, which saps the moral vigor of a race.

I refer to their need for a leader.

While each Cro-Magnon warrior, scout, huntsman, or artisan considers himself the natural equal of every other, and remains independent to a certain degree, the structure of their society is more rigidly authoritarian even than our own. Each man of the tribe belongs to a war party, an allegiance generally inactive save in time of open conflict. And each party has its chieftain. A higher general allegiance is owed to the Omad himself, of course.

Now these men regarded me as their chieftain, and now that I was not with them, they lacked the comforting reassurance of knowing exactly who was in charge. In other words, they needed a clear and unquestioned source of authority: the common purpose alone which they served, that is, to rescue the Professor and myself, was simply not enough. Seldom before in all their lives, save under rare and extraordinary circumstances, had they been utterly alone as now they were. It disheartened them and gnawed away at their morale, and it began to show in certain ways.

Arguments broke out between them over fancied slights. Small, inconsequential arguments, it is true, like the brief exchange of emotionally charged words between Jorn the Hunter and Hurok, but in time, unless corrected, these slights might open fissures between them which would disintegrate their ability to function as a unit.

No clear choice for a leader presented itself: Jorn was too young and hotheaded, Warza too unassuming, and Murg, of course, was hopeless. There remained Parthon and Varak, who were warriors of Sothar, and Ragor and Erdon of the Thandarians.

All, save for the whimpering, conniving little Murg, were brave, strong men. There was little to chose from among them. Nor had I delegated part of my authority to a sub-chieftain, as is sometimes done.

Tacitly, they had yielded to the leadership of Hurok. That is, he had been adamant in his determination to follow after the Dragonmen, and they had, one by one, fallen in with him. But Hurok not only seemed to lack the charisma of leadership, but to the Cro-Magnons it was utterly unthinkable that under any circumstance they would consider one of the feared and despised Drugars their chieftain.

More and more, however, as time passed, they found themselves following Hurok's lead. When he wearied, they rested; when he was hungry, they paused to hunt and eat. It was not that he gave orders or even suggestions. It was simply that, as the strongest and most enduring of them all, when Hurok finally wearied, they, too, were weary. And none of them—saving always for Murg—dared humiliate himself by speaking up and complaining of his hunger or weariness before Hurok admitted the same.

It was a point of honor, you might say.

As for Hurok, he kept his silence, speaking little, as was ever his way. It may have been that the Neanderthal was aware that he had assumed the role of chieftain over the others, without the matter ever being openly spoken of. Or he may simply have done what was natural to him, ignoring the consequences and implications.

As they came nearer to the range of tall mountains which blocked the far end of the plains, the warriors became less open in their movements, proceeding with ever-increasing wariness. There was no telling what lay concealed behind that mighty rampart of living stone, but it seemed to the warriors that the mountains were a natural wall behind which any foe might lie concealed. And the heights and clefts and crevices in that wall afforded excellent natural vantages for whatever sentries might be posted there to guard the approaches to the land of the Dragonmen.

Squatting on their hunkers, hidden in the high grasses, they discussed this question in low tones.

"The spoor of the dragons leads directly thither," Erdon pointed out. "That cleft ahead may well be a pass through the mountains, leading to their country. If so, it will be guarded, for only fools or madmen leave an entryway unwatched."

"Doubtless, Erdon speaks the truth," said Warza briefly. "What then?"

Erdon shrugged, with a grunt of bafflement. His tribe were newcomers to these parts of Zanthodon, having journeyed far up the coast from distant Thandar in search of the lost Princess.

"The men of Sothar are more familiar with this country than are we," said Ragor. "Parthon, Varak—know you aught of what may lie ahead beyond the mountains?"

The two shook their heads.

"When our homeland was destroyed by the earthquakes and the rivers of fire," said Parthon soberly, "we fled toward the sea of Sogar-Jad by another route, falling victim, as you know, to the Gorpaks of the cavern-city. Never has Parthon seen this part of the world before. But we must approach the wall of mountains with great care, keeping ourselves concealed . . . or such, at least, is the advice of Parthon."

"Perhaps we should turn back," whined Murg eagerly. "To rejoin the main body of the tribes and seek the counsels of the Omads, who have wiser heads than any of us."

The others smiled briefly, but made no reply.

Varak whispered to Jorn, who squatted at his side: "Isn't it remarkable how some birds always sing the same tune?" Jorn grinned mischievously, but lowered his eyes when Murg cast an offended glare in their direction.

"Perhaps there is another pass through the mountains," suggested Jorn tentatively. The others shrugged: the question the youth had posed was unanswerable.

Unable to reach a common plan among themselves, the Cro-Magnons turned to Hurok, who squatted in silence a little distance apart from them.

"And what says Hurok of Kor to this?" inquired Varak in tones of affability. He was a likable and good-humored fellow, was Varak, and less subject to the hereditary dislikes and suspicions of his tribesmen.

Hurok said nothing for a time, squinting against the glare of day as he studied the slopes and peaks of the mountain range before them.

"We will not be at the foot of the mountains for at least another wake and sleep," murmured Warza. "And we need not come to a decision until then . . . ?"

"It is best to know what you will do before you do it," grunted Hurok stolidly, measuring the mountains with his eye.

"Then what does Hurok suggest we should do?" demanded Jorn the Hunter.

"Find another way across the mountains than the one before us which was taken by the Dragonmen," said the mighty Neanderthal.

"And . . . if there *is* no other way?" invited Varak.

Hurok gave him an indifferent glance, grunted and spat, as if disgusted by all of this endless talk.

"Climb," he growled.

"*Climb?*" screeched Murg in alarm, his face twitching.

"Climb," repeated Hurok without change of expression.

Murg clutched his bony knees, chewing agitatedly on his lower lip. All too well did he remember the time he had been seized by One-Eye during their flight from the caverns of the Gorpaks, and the breathless and unending horror of the climb down the sheer cliffs which the brutal Drugar had forced upon him. The experience was seared deep in the recollection of Murg, and haunted his dreams even now. He wished mightily that he need never repeat that hair-raising descent . . . and, surely, climbing *up* the wall of a cliff would be every bit as ghastly as climbing *down* one!

The skinny little man groaned and hid his face in his hands. The others grinned slightly but looked away with the simple politeness of their kind, so as not to embarrass Murg. There was ever about the Cro-Magnon a simple rude, unspoken chivalry and decency, even toward those lesser than themselves, who were otherwise viewed as contemptible.

During the next sleep period, Murg lay awake until all the others had dozed off, having rather surprisingly volunteered to take the first watch. As soon as he was positive they all slept deeply, he crawled out of his nest of grasses and purloined the better weapons from the sides of his slumbering comrades.

Gathering up the major part of their supplies of food and water, Murg stole out into the plain and began trotting rapidly in the opposite direction—away from the cliffs.

He could not have known it, but he was traveling with all haste out of the frying pan and right into the middle of the fire.

Chapter 8

A ROYAL INTERVIEW

Before the majordomo (or whatever he was) dared to admit us into the sacrosanct presence of his Empress, he saw to it that we were cleaned up. Female Cro-Magnon slaves bathed and shaved us—or shaved *me*, that is! For the Professor, whose straggly little tuft of chin-whiskers they would have sheared away, raised such a yowl of anguished outrage at the very prospect that, at a hasty wave of one bejewelled hand of the Grand Panjandrum, (or whatever he was), they demurred and permitted him the old fellow to remain in possession of his beloved goatee.

I have had many strange and unusual experiences in my time, some good, plenty bad, most of them inconsequential, but this was the first time since I was a small child that I had to submit to another person's giving me a bath. I felt distinctly foolish during the whole ordeal, although God knows the hot, scented, soapy water looked indescribably delicious and it was bliss to have the dried-on dirt scraped clean from my hide.

The slave women giggled at the expression of grim, mute suffering on my face as they undressed me, plunked me down in the huge marble tub, and began the clean-him-up process. It was not so much that I am prudish about stripping to the buff in the presence of others, even of young women, but there is something damned uncomfortable about just lying there like a hopeless vegetable while other hands than yours scrub your back, douse your hair, and wash even more personal parts—giggling all the while as you flush scarlet with mortification.

I would have made a lousy Roman emperor, I guess.

All cleaned up, clean-shaven, my hair combed, smelling sweet and fixed up with new duds (a scarlet silk loincloth, high-laced buskins of supple, gilt leather, and a hip-length tunic of fine linen), I have to admit I felt like a new man. A rather silly-looking new man, I'm afraid, but a new man nonetheless.

My only comfort came from the fact that Professor Potter looked a lot sillier than I did. The slaves had tied a lilac ribbon in what was left of his wispy white hair, and, with his bony arms and skinny legs sticking out of the tunic, he looked like someone gotten up for a fancy-dress ball.

Once we were all spiffied-up and met the approval of a personal inspection by the Lord High Booleyway (or whatever he was), this important individual led us on neck-tethers through the palace to our impending interview with Royalty. I assumed some notion of the importance of this fat geezer with the perfumed hair from the manner in which everyone we passed while going through the halls and corridors fell hastily on his knees and kowtowed as he went waddling past, ignoring them in his lordly way.

The suites and apartments through which we were led grew ever more sumptuous, as we progressed from the areas given over to mundane pursuits and labors toward those reserved for the aristocracy of the court and the monarch herself. My companion burbled ecstatically over virtually everything in sight.

"Holy Homer! Look at those frescoes, my boy!" he exclaimed, eyes aglow behind his wobbling pince-nez. I looked; they were very handsome, indeed, odd-looking panthers gamboling through a formal garden with droopy trees like willows and lots of amphora-shaped vases standing around on pedestals.

"Ah!—the *mosaics!*" he squealed—we were then crossing a rotunda floored with thousands of tiny bits of tile arranged to depict varieties of marine life, including lobsters, sharks, dolphins, squid, seashells, seaweed, starfish, and so on.

"Very pretty," I commented.

" 'Pretty'!" he snorted, freezing me with a glare. "The mentality that finds this magnificent mosaic floor merely 'pretty' would doubtless consider the Parthenon a 'nice building.' Really, my boy, you have no soul. . . ."

I suppressed a grin, but said nothing.

The Exalted Grand Vizier (or whatever he was) peered loftily at us as the Professor burbled on over the vases, the wall hangings, the silver lamps, and everything else in sight. I suspect that this individual was a trifle mystified to hear us talking in an unknown language (we were speaking English), since everyone else in the Underground World speaks a single common language. Except for the Zarians, as I've already explained, who have retained something like their original Cretan tongue. But the Panjandrum was too exalted to ask a question of a barbarian, obviously. Although he was dying to ask us what the hell was the peculiar lingo we were talking. . . .

We spent what seemed like the better part of an hour cooling our heels in an antechamber to the throne room. The reason for this was that there were an awful lot of people ahead of us in line waiting for an audience with the Sacred Empress. Most of them were courtiers and aristocrats; you could tell this from their garments, which were woven of lustrous silk, with tasseled fringes dyed gold or crimson or purple, and from the amount of jewelry they wore, which was mostly of beaten gold.

The men, that is: as for the women, they wore long ruffled dresses like Victorian women, with many petticoats. Their silken black tresses were teased into frizzy waves or braided into innumerable thin plaits. Some wore little silver bells woven into their hair, which chimed pleasantly as they moved; others wore gems threaded on silver wire.

Rather disconcertingly, they were naked above the waists of these dresses, although a narrow strap went up from the waist to the shoulders, from which fell flounced sleeves of transparent gauzy stuff. I hadn't seen so many nude breasts since my one and only tour of the secret, outlawed slave market in Marrakesh, and I have to admit it was hard not to stare.

The Zarian women, like their Cretan ancestresses, are remarkably handsome, with lustrous black hair, coral lips, superb breasts (the nipples either painted with rouge or brushed with powdered gold), and flashing dark eyes made mysteriously seductive with some cosmetic similar to kohl.

They wear an awful lot of jewelry, as did the men.

As for the Professor, he hastily averted his eyes from this generous display of mammaries—but not before soaking up one long hard look, I assure you!—and twisted his mouth into a sour expression, after giving voice to one disapproving sniff. As for the women, they chattered excitedly, looking us up and down and whispering behind their fans and giggling. One elderly grande dame seemingly took a fancy to the Prof and kept shooting languorous glances at him beneath flutter-

ing, purple-painted lids. When he stiffly declined to notice,
she began pelting him with large unfamiliar blossoms which
stood near to hand in a huge vase of gleaming malachite.

Reddening visibly, the Professor refused to acknowledge
the flirtation. The old lady did not give up, however, to the
delighted amusement of the younger women.

Besides these, there were various merchants or artisans
waiting for judgment on their lawsuits, or something. The
merchants belonged to a lower class, obviously, and were inclined to corpulence. They had double chins, and sometimes
three, and noses more pronouncedly hooked than the aristocrats', and very often their chins were blue-stubbled and un-
shaven, although it was apparent they had donned their
fanciest garments for the interview with Royalty.

Everybody wore entirely too much perfume.

Little pages kept running in and out of the throne room,
bearing messages on small plates of silver. They were Minoans, not Cro-Magnon youngsters, and they were stark
naked except for sandals. Very often they were painted with
cosmetics, including lipstick, and were elaborately coiffed.
With all the nude little boys around, it began to look like the
antechamber to the throne room of Tiberius or Heliogabalus.

My experiences with Royalty have been few and far between. I didn't like what I was seeing: these people seemed
bored, frivolous, perverse, and decadent. The sort that go in
for orgies and gladiatorial games and ambiguous erotic
pleasures.

Give me some honest barbarians, any day of the week.
Even the Gorpaks, for all their cruelties, looked better to me
than these painted, lisping creatures.

The Professor, on the other hand, was making no moral
judgments (not counting his prudery regarding the bare-
breasted ladies). He was taking everything in with a minute
scrutiny, as if trying to memorize every detail—which is
probably exactly what he was doing. The antechamber was, I
have to admit, a splendidly furnished room. The walls were
faced with alabaster and painted with exquisite friezes of
mythological scenes—dancing nymphs, handsome shepherds,
quaint monsters, pagan rites. The furniture was carved from
wood and gilded, luxurious with plump cushions and soft
furs. Perfumed vapors fell from lamps of pierced silver suspended from the beams overhead, and the carpeting—the first
I had seen in Zar—was of thick, lush weave. On small tab-
orets which were scattered about stood ripe fruits in bowls

of electrum, flagons of wine, piles of honeyed cakes, bunches of grapes, shelled nuts—a veritable free lunch.

Guards stood everywhere, stationed motionlessly about the walls, with two huge Cro-Magnon mercenaries, or whatever, to either side of the door which led into the throne room. The doorway was of fretted ivory, hung with a purple length of cloth.

The guards were so immobile that after a while you took them for statues and forgot they were there. But they watched everything, eyes keen and alert beneath the peculiar visors of their gold-washed helmets, which sported scarlet-dyed crests of stiff feathers like the Trojans wear in historical movies.

I gathered the Empress might be a Goddess, but was mortal enough to fear assassination. . . .

One by one the people who had gotten there ahead of us were summoned into the Presence. I kept looking around, wondering what had become of Xask—with a cunning, unscrupulous sneak like him around, you like to have him where you can keep your eyes upon him—but he had been separated from us in the bathing chamber and we hadn't seen him since.

Eventually it was our turn, and we were led into the throne room by the Panjandrum, who strutted importantly to the foot of the dais, very suddenly and quite completely lost all of his importance and fell down on his belly, ground his face into the tiled floor and kissed it humbly, while groveling.

I gathered that much the same performance was expected of the Professor and myself. I'm afraid I had something else to occupy my mind. In fact, I was staring up at the slim figure on the throne with utter amazement written all over my features.

I have never been so absolutely and completely astonished in all of my life—

For there, seated demurely upon the high throne of Zar, sat my beloved Princess—*Darya of Thandar*.

Chapter 9

YUALLA OF SOTHAR

The two tribes continued their long march across the northernmost extremity of the continent, following the coast-line for many sleeps and wakes. The Cro-Magnon warriors had no clear, precise idea of where they were headed, but they knew that they would recognize it when they found it.

They did not, however, find the spoor of the lost Darya nor of my party of warriors. This puzzled them more than a little, but to retrace their steps seemed futile—almost as futile as trying to find our tracks amidst the grassy plains.

Like the true woodsmen they were, the men of Sothar and Thandar lived off the land. Daily—if I may use the term in this world where there is neither night nor day but only a perpetual noon—their scouts and huntsmen spread out, flushing game from the grasses and making their kills with spear or bow.

One of these huntsmen, not surprisingly, was Yualla, the teenaged daughter of Garth, Omad of the Sotharians. I say "not surprisingly," because the women of the Cro-Magnon tribes were not the pampered playthings of their men, nor was the range of their activities limited to such domestic tasks as cooking and child-rearing. Life is hard in this primitive world, filled with hostile tribes and monstrous beasts, and the women learn to hunt and fight and track game as do the men. Frequently, they prove to be better at one or another of these supposedly masculine occupations.

This was the case with Yualla. The girl had demonstrated a keen eye, a steady hand, and a cool nerve when tracking and bringing down game, and she was a dead shot with her bow. Thus, neither the male hunters nor her royal father felt there was anything inappropriate when she volunteered to join the hunting parties.

The truth was, Yualla was bored and restless. She was

60

about Jorn's age, and stunningly attractive, with clear blue eyes and a long, unruly mane of blond hair. Her young body was slim and lithe and supple, the body of a dancer or a gymnast, without a superfluous ounce of flesh. She could run like a deer, climb like a monkey, and fight as well as any boy of her own age.

The only trouble with Yualla was, that, being the Omad's daughter, she was more than a trifle spoiled and accustomed to having her own way. This made her reckless and adventurous, which more than once had gotten her into trouble.

As on the occasion of which I speak. . . .

Under the command of one of the senior huntsmen, a grizzled and veteran warrior named Sarga, Yualla had departed from the camp early that morning with a band of other hunters in search of game. Of which there was certainly a plenitude in these parts, for zomaks nested along the rocky coastline and herds of uld roamed the prairie-like plains.

The uld, by the way, are small, harmless, and quite edible little mammals which resemble fat, short-legged deer. Professor Potter identified them as eohippus, the ancestor (or *an* ancestor) of the modern horse; anyway, they are quite tasty when roasted or broiled.

Quite early during this expedition, the limber, adventure-loving cave-girl had outdistanced her comrades, preferring as always to hunt alone rather than in company. There was hardly a chance of her getting lost, for the plains were wide and flat and the smoke of cookfires from the tribal encampments could be seen a very long distance off. Nor were there any dangerous predators which employed the plains for their own hunting grounds, insofar as the Cro-Magnons knew.

She struck deep toward the center of the plain, following the tracks of a small herd of uld which were scarcely discernible in the thick grasses. Slung over her back, she carried a narrow quiver containing some sixteen flint-bladed arrows; her unstrung bow she carried in her left hand. The only other weapon the cave-girl had with her was a fine bronze knife, a present from her royal father, which had a deerskin scabbard. This she wore tied by thongs to her right thigh.

In the humid and tropical climate which seems to pervade all of this Underground World of Zanthodon, nobody wears much clothing. Hence all the girl wore was a beautifully tanned fawnskin garment resembling a brief apron which covered her slim loins and extended over one shoulder, concealing one pointed young breast and leaving the other bare. A necklace of colored seashells hung about her slender throat, and her feet were shod in supple buskins, laced up to mid-calf.

All the rest of her was naked, clear, golden-tanned, vibrantly beautiful—girl.

Unknown to Yualla of Sothar, another hunter was abroad that day, also on the track of the tasty and defenseless little herd of uld. This second hunter was one of the most fearsome of all of the predators of Zanthodon, the dreaded thakdol—the mighty pterodactyl of the dim Jurassic.

Aloft on its batlike, membranous wings, the flying lizard floated against the golden glow which permeated the misty skies of this primitive world like some monster out of nightmare. With its fanged, elongated jaws (which were not unlike those of the alligator or crocodile), its horrible bird-clawed feet, its long and snaky tail, the thakdol was hideous to behold—and every bit as dangerous and deadly as it was hideous.

It was not long before the minuscule brain of the thakdol saw and recognized the tiny figure far below as something edible. Not as tasty or as defenseless as the uld, of course, but the aerial monster had eaten of human flesh many times ere this, and found the dish to its liking.

The intelligence of the dragon of the skies was dim and rudimentary, for the pterodactyl was virtually nothing more than a murder machine, a flying stomach. And its minute brain could only contain one thought at a time. Up until this moment that peanut-sized organ had entertained naught but the idea of uld . . . tempting, juicy, squealing, fat uld. Thus at first, and for some little time thereafter, the thakdol ignored the running figure beneath it as irrelevant to its fixation on uld-hunting.

But in time the notion filtered into the dim brain of the flying reptile that the cave-girl would easily provide it with the luncheon it hungered for, and the idea of *girl* began to take dominance over that of *uld*.

It was perhaps too much to ask of the thakdol's rudimentary brain to expect it to weigh its chances. The pterodactyl well knew from former encounters that, as often as not, the two-legged prey bore sharply pointed sticks with which they were accustomed to thrust and jab at the tender bellies of such as it. And, on other occasions, they had been known to wield heavy stone axes, or to loose from stringed sticks flying slivers of wood that could be an annoyance, even a bother.

No, the thakdol was hunting, and it was hungry. And when this happened, it simply took wing from its mountaintop aerie and hunted until it found something to kill. Then it feasted.

However, some instinctive element of caution may have awakened within the brain of the flying reptile. For, although it could not have known this, the running girl as yet remained ignorant of the thakdol's existence.

Thus when it folded those broad, batlike wings and fell out of the skies like a plummet, the girl did not realize her danger until it was too late for her to defend herself.

A hideous black shadow fell over her. Throwing back her head, Yualla stared with a thrill of incredulous horror at the fanged monstrosity which hurtled toward her out of the heavens. There was no time to string the bow she held, no time to loose so much as a single arrow at that mailed breast. The winged monster would pounce upon her in another breath: already its clawed feet were spread, ready to rip and rend her tender flesh—

Yualla did the only thing possible—she threw herself flat and rolled into the thick grasses. It was a vain hope, that of hiding herself among the grasses, but it was all that she had. And, as it happened, it was probably the wisest thing she could have done, under such circumstances.

For the thakdol hunts as the eagle hunts, swooping out of the sky to snatch its prey into the air. And, lying close against the flat earth as she was, the cave-girl presented the hardest possible target for those terrible claws. Thus, when the bird descended, it was forced to hang on beating vans while scrabbling about for her slender form, which it could not see because she was underneath it and its own body blocked its view.

Breathless, with furiously beating heart, the girl rolled this way and that upon the meadow, striving to elude the clutches of those horrible, hooked claws, and narrowly succeeding.

But then one claw closed by accident about her lower leg. It caught her above the ankle of one foot, and, as it chanced, when the claw snapped shut like a curved trap, it closed and curled about the limb but did not bite into it.

Sensing that it had seized its prey, the thakdol instantly

"The fanged monstrosity hurtled toward her."

rose, raising a dust storm from the beating of its mighty wings.

As it rose into the air, it dragged the helpless girl with it.

By a miracle, the girl was as yet uninjured. Had the reptile ascended with the swooping flight that had been its original intention, the shock would doubtless have broken Yualla's leg. But now it rose from an almost stationary posture, slowly and laboriously due to the girl's weight, and thus the ascent was slower than it might have been. And Yualla had the presence of mind—which was remarkable, under such circumstances—to dangle loosely and limply, rather than to kick or struggle.

Through it all, she had somehow managed to hang onto her bow. So the blond cave-girl was not unarmed, although there was little she could do to fight in her present awkward position. She was, after all, hanging head down.

For an instant, she entertained the wild notion of trying to put an arrow through the belly of the brute, which was directly above her and exposed and vulnerable. But already the plain was swaying and dwindling beneath her as the monster gained the upper air, and long before she could have strung the bow and nocked an arrow, she was too high. To have fallen from such a height as this would have killed her instantly.

Flapping on slow and laboring wings, burdened by the weight of its captive, the thakdol flew off across the plain in the direction of that range of mountains which led to Zar, in whose peaks its nest was concealed.

Chapter 10

ZARYS OF ZAR

Identical in every respect with my lost Princess, the beautiful woman on the throne stared down at me with surprise—and with some other emotion I could not at once identify—in her wide and innocent blue eyes.

There was no question about it—the Empress of Zar was none other than Darya of Thandar! Although how this impossible thing could ever be was a mystery defying my solution at that time.

The long slim legs, the superb, pointed breasts, the magnificent mane of curling golden hair, framing the clear oval of that lovely, flower-like face—all, all were Darya's.

But, whereas my Princess had gone clad in abbreviated furs, her small feet buskin-shod, crude jewelry clasped at throat and wrist, this magnificent woman was one blaze of jewels.

Clasped about the base of her throat, a yoke of gems threaded on crimson silk clad her upper torso, rising and falling with her lovely, half-naked breasts. Suspended from the terminals of this pectoral yoke, long silken threads, strung with gems, fell to veil but not conceal the exquisite lines of her belly and hips and slim thighs. It was with a distinct shock that I saw, beneath this incredible garment of jewels, she was utterly nude.

"Who is this barbarian," she demanded imperiously, "who seems to recognize us, but upon whom our eyes have never laid—and why does he insolently stand erect, when all men kneel in our presence?"

The moment she spoke, I knew that she could not be the Darya I had known. My beloved Princess spoke with clear, soft, bell-like tones and silvery chiming laughter; this woman's voice was throaty, husky, deep, with a seductive purr behind its music.

"Divine Zarys, I shall bend those stubborn knees," rumbled a bass voice. A burly, dwarfish man clad in golden greaves and glittering breastplate strode from his station at the foot of the dais, glaring at me.

I was too dazed with shock to think straight or to move. As the gorgeously caparisoned officer came strutting up to me and made as if to club me over the head with his black enamel baton, I merely balled one fist and sank it into his solar plexus with all my strength.

There was, you see, a gap between the bottom of the cuirass and the ornate buckle of the heavy girdle which clasped his waist. It was about the size of my fist, I calculated.

It was, too.

He staggered as if he had walked into an invisible wall, purpled, then turned pale as curdled milk, and sagged to his knees, metal greaves clanking on the tiles. Then he lost his lunch rather noisily.

I filed away for future reference the interesting fact that the Minoan Cretans, despite their urban sophistication and remarkable advances, remained ignorant of the fine art of pugilism.

The Empress made a sound of disgust and rose from her throne, striding down the steps of the dais like a glittering waterfall of gems, fastidiously avoiding her sprawled and vomiting officer, and strode through a curtained doorway into an inner chamber.

I gathered that the audience was over.

And, from the murderous glare I received from the officer I had knocked down, I gathered my life was to be reckoned in minutes, or however long it would take him to get through with being sick.

One of his lieutenants helped him stagger to his feet. Another wiped his lips and chin with a corner of his cloak. I guessed the man was a personage of some considerable prominence, from the way toadies and underlings hurried to fawn about him, shoot me frosty glares, and tut-tut over his "accident."

"Ialos, lend me your sword," he said thickly.

With a gloating smile in my direction, his lieutenant made haste to put the weapon into his hand.

Stiff-legged as a barnyard rooster whose private henhouse has been invaded by another rooster, the man I had hit came toward me. I balled my two fists and prepared to give him a second lesson in the fine art of fisticuffs. As it turned out, the opportunity did not come.

A slim dark girl in diaphanous silks, who had come silently up behind him, laid one hand on his brawny forearm.

"General Cromus, your revenge must wait upon another time, for the Goddess will see this barbarian privately," she said in a soft, lisping voice.

Cromus froze, licked his lips, stared at me with hot, hating eyes, and reluctantly returned the weapon to his underling.

All this time, the pudgy Grand Panjandrum (I soon discovered him to be the Royal Chamberlain, and his name turned out to be Hissab) and the Professor remained facedown on the tiled floor, neither daring to move. Hissab now inched his head about and stared at me with blank astonishment. I judged that private audiences were seldom awarded, and never to unruly barbarians. I tipped the fat man a wink which seemed to scandalize him.

The girl came up to me, eyeing me from head to foot admiringly.

"This way," she said demurely, leading me off.

Beyond the portal lay a small, dainty, rosy-lit room which seemed to serve as the retiring room of the Empress. When I came in, following the girl sent to fetch me, her maids were in the process of assisting their monarch to disrobe. The jeweled collar had been unclasped, baring to my view her beautiful breasts, and the fabulous garment slid away showing me rather more naked girlflesh than I was comfortable at seeing.

The Empress, after one indifferent glance in my direction, continued to submit to being undressed by the maids, who stored the robe of jewels carefully away in a chest of carven wood painted with octopi and seashells. The naked woman ignored my presence as if I were a pet dog.

I was intrigued; also, if I was a little affronted. Women, especially when naked, tend not to ignore me.

One of the maids gently adjusted a gauzy robe about the shoulders of her mistress. This clasped only at the throat, opening all the way down whenever she moved, so the view continued to be a distraction. Also, the robe was about as transparent as a veil of smoke, so none of the attractions were all that concealed from my eyes. But I felt a little more comfortable, somehow.

Then she glided across the fur rugs to curl up on a sofa which was piled with many small, plump, bright-colored cushions. She then calmly regarded me with faint curiosity in her eyes, as well as that emotion I had glimpsed before. Was it—admiration? Or was I flattering myself?

"Does the animal speak a civilized tongue?" the Empress asked.

The girl who had come to fetch me said: "According to the Lord Chamberlain, Divine Mistress, the creature is not unproficient in our tongue."

"Remarkable," drawled the woman on the sofa. Then she patted the cushions at her side and ordered (or invited? It was hard to tell) me to sit at her side.

I did so, a bit gingerly. We looked each other over with frank curiosity.

Up close like this, I noticed subtle differences between Zarys and Darya which had been invisible at first look. The Empress used cosmetics. Something like kohl darkened her long lashes, discreet use of paints made her eyelids mysterious and shadowy blue, accenting her superb eyes, and a scarlet cream reddened her full, seductive lips.

Since she was virtually naked, I could not help noticing other differences, as well. Darya was slim and lean, deliciously curved where nature designed women to be deliciously curved, and firmly muscled as a boy, without an ounce of fat.

The Empress of Zar, on the other hand, was softer and rounder, and just the slightest bit more svelt than Darya. She was also, I think, three or four years older, and there was a trace of petulance around her mouth and a hardness in her gaze, an arrogance, which Darya did not have. Still and all, the resemblances between them were astonishing: twin sisters could not have been more alike than the two women.

"Palaika," murmured the Empress, tossing her head. One of the maids came gliding over and, with a distinct shock, I watched her take off the wig.

Yes, that glorious curling mane of golden hair was a wig! I was appalled: beneath the wig (which was of gold wire, spun finer than silk thread), the Empress's head was shaven bald.

Somehow, it did not make her any the less gorgeous. . . . Later, I came to understand that the palace aristocrats of Zar were all alike, slim, olive-skinned, black haired. They prized and hungered after novelty, and the current fashion was to emulate the beauty of the Cro-Magnon slave women, who were, of course, blonde. I have never understood where Zarys got her big blue eyes from—perhaps from some antique My-

cenaean Greek ancestor in the remote past—but her golden
hair was nothing but a golden wig.

"Is it true you are acquainted with our language?" she
asked me curiously. I stammeringly said something to the effect that I was beginning to pick it up a little. My barbaric
accent made her wrinkle up her nose, but my uncomfortable
expression made her smile mischievously—and she looked
more like Darya than ever. They had the same smile!

"In the Pasiphaeum you seemed to recognize me, yet you
are not of our race, and a stranger to our realm. How is
this?"

" 'Pasiphaeum'?" I repeated.

She shrugged impatiently. "As a direct descendant of the
Goddess Pasiphae, wife of the Divine Minos, I . . . but here
I am answering a slave's questions, and him a barbarian as
well! Answer me: you seemed to recognize me. How?"

"Well, uh," I began; and falteringly I tried to explain about
Darya and how much they resembled each other. She seemed
intrigued at being the mirror image of a Cro-Magnon girl,
rather than being offended by the comparison.

"I see," she murmured. "You were, when captured by the
Outriders who guard the approaches to my realm, in the
company of the despicable Xask, exiled former prince of the
city; how is this?"

"Accident, more than anything else. He is my enemy as
well as yours, your majesty."

A pouting smile touched those full red lips.

" 'My majesty' . . . how quaint! But my subjects generally
give me the title Divinity or Goddess . . . my name, however, is Zarys. Do barbarians of your tribe have given
names?"

I was getting just a little tired of being called a barbarian.
However, I held my temper and told her my name.

"Eric Carstairs," she repeated. "How uncouth a name . . .
nonetheless, it seems to suit you."

She caressed me slowly with her eyes, her expression demure, a tantalizing smile playing about her mouth. I flushed a
little as she looked me over, feeling like a prize bull on display at a cattle auction. At the same time, I felt her nearness
powerfully: she was so very much like my lost beloved that I
ached to seize her in my arms, to crush her against my chest,
to cover her flower-like face with my hot, panting kisses.

And something of what I was feeling must have shown in

my eyes, for she smiled a slow languorous smile and touched me gently on the thigh.

"We shall speak again, Eric Carstairs, at dinner . . ."

I was led out, feeling absurdly as if I had narrowly escaped what the authors of Victorian melodrama would have called A Fate Worse Than Death.

Part Three

ACROSS THE PLAINS

Chapter 11

MURG IS MISSING

They were eating their breakfast, camped on the plain, when Ragor noticed that Murg was missing from their number. The Thandarian mentioned the fact to his brother-warrior, Erdon.

"Sometime as we slept, it seems, our friend Murg decided to seek the greater safety that lies in numbers," said Ragor, nodding. "There; see? His few possessions are gone, and he himself is nowhere to be seen."

Erdon grunted, unimpressed by the urgency of the news. "So that is what has become of my water bottle," he muttered. "And of my spare sandals!"

The two Cro-Magnons grinned at each other briefly.

"If we speak of this to the others, Hurok may decide to turn back and seek the little man," Ragor pointed out.

"That is so. Let us say nothing, then. After all, Murg was no good in a fight, and of no use in the hunt, so he will hardly be missed, even by his fellow tribesmen."

They decided to say nothing of their discovery. A bit later, Varak of Sothar came up to where they sat.

"I have lost my best dagger," he complained. "The one with the obsidian blade and the handle made of thantor ivory. Has either of you seen it lying about?"

By thantor, he referred to the woolly mammoth.

"Ragor has seen naught of the dagger belonging to Varak," said that worthy.

"Neither has Erdon," grunted Erdon.

Varak looked nonplussed. "It was my best dagger," he said in grieved tones. "The blade withstood nicks better even than the bronze knife which Hurok carries tucked in his furs—the one he took from the Gorpak captain back in the cavern city."

"That is too bad," said Erdon. "I, too, have lost something—my water bottle of greased leather."

Varak scratched his jaw with his thumbnail. "I don't understand it! Surely, we have no thief amongst us. . . ."

"Not any longer, anyway," grinned Ragor.

Varak, puzzled, asked, "What do you mean by that?"

Ragor chuckled. "Look around you. As we slept, your friend Murg stole off, presumably hoping to rejoin our two tribes. And that's not all he stole; doubtless, his disappearance serves to explain the vanishing of your dagger."

"Murg, is it?" growled Varak angrily. "No friend of mine—my best dagger!" Then he paused to reflect. "Well . . . at least we shall be able to make better time from here on. I never saw a man who got more thorns in his foot and needed to pause to remove the offending object from his sensitive flesh. But why have you said nothing to the others of this?"

Erdon shrugged. "Hurok may wish to turn back and find him. Our Drugar friend is excessively tender hearted—for a Drugar. And I would much rather rescue Eric Carstairs and Professor Potter, than rescue Murg. Let the little whimpering weakling fend for himself. Perhaps he will be eaten by a xunth," he added, smiling.

"Or a thakdol," suggested Varak.

"Even an uld could do the trick," laughed Ragor.

Breaking camp, the small war party continued the journey. They had reached the foothills before the range of mountains, and were skirting their flanks, seeking for a way over the immense barrier. They saw nothing of the guards and sentinels of Zar, but, then, guards and sentinels are stationed to see and not to be seen. Neither did they see aught of any dangerous predators, save for a number of thakdols which nested amid the peaks above and who could be seen flapping and circling about the sky.

If Hurok noticed that Murg was missing from their number, he said nothing about it to anyone. It is, of course, the duty of a leader (even a *de facto* leader like Hurok) to assume the responsibility for his men, even those who are unpopular, or, as in the case of Murg, heartily detested. One presumes, from his actions, or, rather, from his lack of actions, that Hurok was more concerned with the safety of Black Hair and his elderly friend than he was with the safety of Murg.

After several hours, during which the war party continued north along the mountain-guarded borders of the land of Zar, the sharp eyes of Varak the Sotharian succeeded in spying a cleft between two mountains which turned out on closer inspection to be a pass across the mountains. It was somewhat narrower than the well-guarded pass of the stone dragon-head, and it would be much more difficult to traverse, but it was better than trying to scale one of the mountain peaks.

After a brief pause to rest, and with Hurok in the lead, the warriors entered the foothills and began to ascend the flanks of the mountain toward the mouth of the little pass. The ground was covered with broken, loose rocks, the detritus of centuries of erosion and landslides, and the going was slow and difficult. But none of the men made complaint about this.

"If Murg were here, he would be complaining of a pebble in his sandal by now," remarked Ragor to Varak.

"If Murg were here he would have done so long before this," grinned Varak.

Hurok, whose eyesight might be dim but whose huge ears missed nothing, grunted a retort to the two warriors.

"Since Murg is not here, Hurok suggests that Varak and Ragor save their breath for climbing," advised the massive Neanderthal.

The two nodded guiltily and climbed with redoubled vigor.

As for the object of their humor, poor little Murg had spent a miserable "night." The dwarfish Sotharian had seldom felt so completely alone in his life, and did not enjoy the experience in the slightest. Burdened as he was with the supplies and extra weapons he had purloined from his erstwhile comrades, the homely little man made very poor time in crossing the plain. Moreover, weariness assailed him; a succession of jaw-cracking yawns drew to his attention that he was intolerably sleepy. But to curl up alone amidst the waste was to fall prey to the very first hungry predator that came roaming by in search of a midnight snack.

Unhappily, Murg decided to go on. He wanted to put as much distance between himself and the others as possible before they awoke. He had a well-developed imagination for a caveman, and could envision all too well the punishment that would be sternly meted out to him should he again encounter the warriors from whom he had thieved.

Too sleepy to go on and too frightened to fall asleep, Murg faced quite a troublesome dilemma. Whining and sniffling and grumbling to himself, the little fellow staggered on through the thick grasses, burdened down by all the extra rations of food, the sleeping hides, the weapons and water bottles he had stolen before making his hasty escape from the camp.

To risk sleep, thus risking being eaten alive? To continue his journey, weary though he was? Which course should he follow? The question, to his exhausted mind, seemed insoluble.

Fortunately—for him, if not for another—Fate quickly solved Murg's problem for him.

And in so doing, presented him with yet another problem! But, then, that is one of Fate's little tricks.

A black shadow fell across Murg as he trudged along, whimpering miserably to himself. He looked up and saw a monstrous thakdol descending toward him on ragged, batlike wings.

With a squeal of terror, Murg flung down the load he was carrying and picked up his heels to run for safety. Almost at once he tripped over a root and fell face down in the thick grasses.

Dust blew about him as the pterodactyl descended to earth. Cowering in the grasses with both hands firmly clamped over his eyes, Murg shuddered, awaiting his doom.

The thakdol rose after a moment and flapped away. Eyes squeezed shut, Murg dared neither move nor breathe, momentarily expecting to be eaten up.

But nothing happened.

Then—and *very* unexpectedly—the toe of a sandal prodded him in his bony ribs.

Squawking in fear, Murg rolled over on his back, knees doubled up to protect his fat little belly. Although what possible protection those skinny knees could have afforded against the hook-like claws of a thakdol, even Murg could not have explained.

"Don't eat me, don't eat me!" begged Murg in a tremulous voice, eyes still squeezed shut.

"I won't," said a girl's voice in somewhat impatient and shaky tones, "but I may have to kick your ribs in before you give me your attention."

Astounded, Murg opened his eyes and stared up into the face of a lovely blonde girl who was about the last person he would have expected to see here in the northern parts of the plain. It was, of course, Yualla.

"Wh-what is Yualla the gomad doing here?" he quavered in utter amazement.

The girl shrugged, ill-humoredly. "For that matter," she countered, "what is Murg doing here?"

The thakdol which had carried the cave-girl off had not been fully grown, it seems. One of the flying lizards in the full prime of its strength could have borne her away to its mountaintop nest with relative ease. But the half-grown brute wearied erelong of its burden and descended to the surface of the plain to rest.

Probably, it had planned to devour its captive there on the plain, and to regurgitate the meal later into the clacking beaks of its hungry offspring—if offspring it had.

At any rate, Yualla, who had kept her wits about her, made use of the first opportunity that came along. As the claws opened to drop her, the limber girl whirled in midair, landing on her feet as lightly as a cat.

Disconcerted, the pterodactyl peered at her with first one eye and then the other. It was not used to prey which remained unaccountably alive. Making a tentative pass at the blonde girl with one cruel claw, the reptile received an arrow through its upper leg in result. For Yualla had not dropped her bow during her inadvertent voyage through the upper air.

This was too much for the tired, hungry, and more than a little confused young thakdol. Rising hastily on flapping wings, it circled off in search of more amenable prey, leaving Yualla alone on the plain.

Or so she first assumed. Until, of course, she spotted Murg cowering amid the grasses, trembling like a leaf and moaning with fear.

Shrugging exasperatedly, the girl strolled over and kicked him in his scrawny ribs, with the resultant brief conversation quoted above. Lost amidst the plains though she was, at least she was not alone or defenseless.

Not that Murg would have been the companion of her choice, had she been given a choice.

Chapter 12

A BANQUET
IN NEW CRETE

Following my brief interview with the Empress, one of her hand-maidens led me back into the throne room where I rejoined the Professor and Hissab, the Grand Panjandrum. General Cromus was still there, being tended by his sycophants. All of the other courtiers and guards were there, too, since the Empress had neither dismissed them nor officially terminated the audience.

I discovered how quickly one can rise in popularity here in Zar. When, that is, one has just spent thirty minutes alone with the Divine Zarys.

The guards and courtiers fawned upon me. An ivory chair was fetched for me. Wine and a tray of goodies were handed to me by sleek, smiling, clean-shaven men. Beautiful women with naked breasts fluttered their long eyelashes in my direction and bathed me from head to foot with admiring, flirtatious glances.

Even Cromus, who purpled with fury at the sight of me, forced a feeble welcoming smile—although the cold venom in his eyes belied it.

"Well, Eric, my boy!" said the Professor, breathing a sigh of relief. "I see you have survived your ordeal . . . I was uncertain whether you were being led away for instant execution or to some sort of, ahem!, a 'male harem.' But here you are, alive and well, and most obviously the hero of the hour. . . ."

"I wouldn't rule out either the execution or the harem bit yet, Doc," I grinned, downing a gulp of the purple wine and biting into a seed-crusted honey cake. The wine was overly sweet to my taste, and had rose leaves floating in it, or petals anyway. But the little cakes tasted fine.

The Grand Panjandrum came ambling over to where I sat, his plump face wreathed with oily smiles. His little slitted eyes, I noticed, however, were shrewd and calculating.

"The Lord Hissab rejoices that the distinguished barbarian has found favor in the eyes of the Immortal Zarys," he said smoothly, ducking his head in the tiniest possible bow. "All the while it was the most earnest hope of this individual that the Goddess might well find her newest guest an interesting and attractive addition to the court. . . ."

"I just bet it was," I said with a grin. Then my grin widened, for across the room, under guard, Xask stood, face grim. He shot me a glance of the purest malignancy, and my grin turned into a chuckle. My sudden rise in status had put the slimy little villain off his stride; he had planned, I have no doubt, to make a grandstand play before the throne, bragging how he had maneuvered me into the grasp of Zar, and displaying the automatic with a splendid flourish, boasting of how his loyalty to his Empress was such that he was ready to lay at her exquisite feet the thunder-weapon which would conquer the Underground World for Zar.

Now, suddenly, his plans had gone awry. The Empress had not even noticed him, and I was almost elevated to the position of Royal Favorite—all because I had intrigued her curiosity with my astonishment at seeing her, and had knocked General Cromus on his keester with a single blow.

The same thought must have flashed through Xask's seething brain in the identical instant, for he turned a thoughtful and appraising glance in the direction of that fine fellow, and a small thin-lipped smile played about the corners of his mouth.

I might have made a very powerful friend in the last few minutes . . . but I had also made a rather dangerous enemy.

He glanced in my direction, caught my eye, and smiled one of those bland, cunning smiles of his.

Oh, we understood ourselves perfectly, Xask and I!

No more slave pens for the likes of the Professor and me; we were moved into a sumptuous suite of apartments which opened upon a small walled garden. The rooms were handsomely furnished with many low, silken divans, heaps of cushions, oddly shaped but not uncomfortable chairs, small tabourets and huge hassocks.

Soft carpets of glowing colors and bold maritime designs lay piled underfoot. Charming frescoes of nymphs and fauns at play in Arcadian woodland glens adorned the plastered walls. Lamps of fretted brass and silver depended from long chains. In them, perfume-impregnated oils burned, shedding a soft glow of light and a rich incense.

"Quite a pad," I remarked, looking around. "Better than the slave pens of the cavern-city, at any rate!"

"There's no question about *that*, my boy!" the Professor chuckled, sinking into one of the divans with bliss written across his features. "So long as we, I mean *you*, can manage to stay in the good graces of the Queen, we shall be living in the veritable lap of luxury. . . ."

"And eating pretty high off the hog, as well," I informed him. "Forgot to mention it, but we've been invited to a royal banquet tonight."

"Which will further serve to discomfort your friend Cromus, to say nothing of our old comrade, Xask," he mused. "We are in dangerous waters, my boy, and I hope you realize the fact! Imperial courts like this are a seething hotbed of Byzantine intrigues, plots and counter-plots and . . . well, all that sort of thing. But—Sainted Schliemann, what an opportunity! There is not an archaeologist alive who would not sell his soul for a chance like this! To observe at first hand the people of Minoan Crete, their customs and traditions, crafts and arts, daily life. . . . It is very like being equipped with Mr. Wells's Time Machine, and voyaging back nearly four thousand years to Knossus at its height . . . !"

"You really think these people are still living the way their ancient ancestors lived, Doc?" I asked skeptically. "Any reasons why they couldn't have changed, progressed, over all those centuries? I mean, look at our Cro-Magnon friends, the warriors of Thandar and Sothar: they made it on their own out of the Stone Age, discovering how to make copper and bronze and Lord knows what else."

"That is true enough, Eric," he said, pursing his lips judiciously. "Under the pressure of adversity, battling against the beasts and rival tribes of Zanthodon, our Cro-Magnon friends rose to the occasion and advanced, I think, rather remarkably. But the Cretans were decadent even back in the days of Knossus, and here on their island-city they are almost completely insulated from the perils and monsters of the Underground World, walled away behind that range of mountains, guarded by their wide moat . . . the motifs of their frescoes and mosaics, the ornamentation on their urns and vases, their modes of dress, even their architectural styles, are one and the same with those uncovered from the ruins of Knossus by Sir Arthur Evans. I very much doubt if the people of Zar have altered their life-style significantly in all this time."

"Well, we'll have to wait and see, I guess."

That night the royal banquet proved to be like something out of a Cecil B. DeMille movie epic. There were dancing girls in skimpy garments, lithe acrobats, clowns, twanging but not unharmonious music played on odd little bagpipes, lutes or harps or something like that, small brightly colored drums, and chimes and cymbals.

We reclined on sumptuous couches, decked out in long-sleeved robes, hand-fed by kneeling slaves. I couldn't begin to tell you what we ate, but every dish was saturated with herbs and spices until we gave up trying to identify the source.

There were little cubes of meat on long skewers with raw onions in between, just like shish kebab; thirty kinds of soups and stews and broths and ragouts; pastries made to look like squid and sharks and dolphins; jellied fruits and honey-hearted wines and preposterous sherbets built out of shaved ice and soaked in fruit juices; and, above all, there was seafood, seafood, seafood.

Crete used to be the major sea power of the ancient Mediterranean, and the Zarians have never forgotten it.

Cromus was there, and so was Hissab, and some of the courtiers I recognized from the throne room, but everyone else was a stranger to me as I was to them. Gossip had gotten around, however, and the men all smiled and waved when I happened to look in their direction, while the women flirted and ogled me, whispering to each other about me behind their feather fans. I felt distinctly uncomfortable, but this was the first truly civilized meal I had enjoyed during all the weeks or months I had spent in Zanthodon, and I tackled it with gusto.

Zarys sat across from me, reclining on a silken couch being fanned by two stalwart blond Cro-Magnon slaves in very brief scarlet loincloths. She wore a long gown with deep sleeves made of some soft crinkly stuff that began at the shoulders as salmon pink and deepened in hue as you went down, until the hem was royal purple. This time the golden wig was gone and her exquisite skull wore a tall headdress that was one glittering mass of blue-white diamonds.

Her breasts were bare but this time the nipples had been painted with liquid gold.

Outside of a languorous glance or two in my direction, she more or less ignored me, placidly permitting herself to be fed. I was just as pleased to be ignored, and busied myself with filling my belly.

After one long murderous glare at me, Cromus ignored me. He wore his gilt armor and a scarlet-plumed headdress, rather like an Indian chief's, and looked grand, I must admit. But he was still quite a bit out of sorts; I could tell he was holding his temper under control, and just barely, because when one of the slave girls—a timid little thing with huge frightened eyes and a shy manner—spilled a little wine, he slapped her resoundingly and angrily wiped the dribble off his chin, brusquely demanding to be served by a less clumsy slave for the rest of the meal.

I could gladly have knocked him down again for that, but I controlled the impulse.

After dinner, slaves snuffed out the candelabra, plunging the windowless room into thick gloom, which was a real novelty here in the Underground World. Then a troupe of dancers came in stark naked, their lithe limbs, bare breasts, and long slender legs painted with some phosphorescent substance so that they glowed with weird colors in the dark. It was a gorgeous dance, I have to admit.

Although, as things turned out, I didn't get to see very much of it. Because, just as we were settling down to watch the luminous dancers, a girl touched me on the wrist. I turned around, recognizing the Empress's handmaiden, the one called Ialys.

She laid her fingertip across my lips as they parted to ask her what was up.

Obeying her tug on my sleeve, I got up and followed her through the darkened room. Whether or not anybody besides the Professor happened to notice me go, I've no idea.

At the doorway, I asked her what was up. She smiled kittenishly, with demurely downcast eyes.

"The Divine Zarys awaits you for a private audience," the girl whispered.

Here it comes, I thought with a sinking heart.

And I was right, too. . . .

Chapter 13

SUNDERED PATHS

From his place amid the plain, Sarga the huntsman watched with horror as the monstrous flying reptile carried away the limp, dangling body of the princess of his tribe.

The grizzled veteran had followed the spoor of Yualla of Sothar when the headstrong girl had decided to strike out on her own in quest of game. He knew very well her reckless, adventuresome ways, having watched her grow from childhood. Partly, he admired her for her contempt of danger and her skills at tracking game, which were qualities he might heartily have desired to discover in any son of his; but, as she was his responsibility as chief of the hunting party, he grimly dreamed of turning her over his knee (or whatever the Cro-Magnon equivalent of a good spanking is) and giving her a lesson in obedience.

When the thakdol descended upon her, Sarga was very far away from where Yualla was—too far away even for his bow to send a feathered shaft. And the pterodactyl had borne the blonde girl into the skies before even his fleet foot could bring him near enough to fight in her defense.

Now, with a sinking heart and a feeling of utter helplessness, he stood and watched as the winged dragon bore the girl aloft. From his distance, even the keen eyes of Sarga could not tell whether it was a living girl the thakdol carried off or a mangled corpse. But somehow Sarga did not quite believe that Yualla had been slain, for all that she hung limply from those cruel claws. He knew her well enough to know that Yualla would have fought with every skill at her command rather than yield supinely to the thakdol's attack. And no sounds of battle had reached his ears.

Marking with his gaze the direction in which the reptile slowly flew on flapping wings, heavily burdened by its prey, the huntsman lifted to his lips the hollowed aurochs horn he

wore belted at his waist and sounded a call. Shortly there
came to him through the long grasses the others of his hunting party, summoned from their stalking by the signal. In
swift, blunt words Sarga made known to them what had just
occurred, and indicated the direction in which the pterodactyl
had carried Yualla.

"Doubtless the thakdols nest in the peaks of that range of
mountains in the distance," he remarked. "It is the nature of
such beasts to bear to their nesting place their kill, to be
devoured at leisure or to be fed to their young."

"If the gomad Yualla has been slain, O Sarga, it makes no
difference in which direction her corpse was carried," reasoned one of the younger hunters. A cold smile touched the
lips of the older man.

"But if the gomad Yualla lives, then it makes all the difference in the world," he pointed out.

"What, then, shall we do?" demanded another of the party.

"We shall return to the encampment of the tribes and
bring these sad matters to the attention of the Omad Garth,"
said Sarga. "As to that which will transpire thereafter, it is up
to the Omad to make the decision. Come, let us begone with
what little game we have managed thus far to procure."

Wasting as little time as possible, the hunting party returned to camp and found Garth of Sothar and his mate in
conversation with one of the warriors of the Thandarians.
They were discussing the direction and the duration of that
day's march, but the conversation was swiftly terminated as
soon as Sarga had informed his chief of what had happened.

The brows of Garth of Sothar darkened thunderously and
he set his jaw grimly against any display of emotion which
might appear unmanly. But those who stood nearby could not
help but notice that he balled his fists with great force, as if
crushing the throat of an enemy. So tightly did Garth of
Sothar clench his mighty fists that blood spurted from
beneath the nails.

His mate, Nian, stood nearby—a handsome, strong woman
just past the blush of her first youth, fit mate for the mighty
jungle monarch. At the sad news which Sarga related, she
paled and bit her lip, but said nothing. She held her head
proudly high, but involuntary tears welled up behind her blue
eyes.

The Cro-Magnons of Zanthodon are, of course, true savages in the finest sense of the word. That is, they are primi-

tives with a rich but simple and thriving culture, their vigor and emotional honesty unencumbered by the accretions of custom and tradition imposed by so-called "civilization." Unlike us of the Western world, they are not ashamed of their emotions, any more than they are ashamed to bare their bodies before others, as prudery and the puritanical repressions of civilization as yet do not constrict their natural responses. There is, I suppose, much about them that would seem shocking to a native of New York or London. The women nonchalantly bare their breasts and both sexes freely employ the great outdoors for their sanitary needs, in lieu of toilets. But let me assure you that there is much about our urban way of life that would seem shocking to the citizens of Thandar or Sothar—our denial of natural emotions, our sense of shame, our repression of the animal instincts, and the ways we cover our bodies and fear and shun the wilderness.

What I am attempting to explain is that it is as common to see a Cro-Magnon male burst into tears over the loss of a comrade as it is to see a Cro-Magnon woman defend her hearth and brood against marauders with a battle-axe. But the High Chief of a tribe, and his mate as well, hold themselves proudly before the eyes of all as an example of stoicism, dignity, and courage. Thus Garth and Nian bore themselves bravely under the shock of Yualla's loss.

Within mere moments, mastering his emotions, Garth had elicited from his huntsman the essential facts surrounding the disappearance of his daughter. Nor did Sarga neglect to advise him of the precise direction in which the pterodactyl had flown, and of the conjectures voiced at the time about its probable destination. The Omad of Sothar was familiar with the habits of thakdols and knew as well as did Sarga that hunting pterodactyls generally carry their prey back to their nests and that they generally nest on mountain peaks, such as those dimly visible across the breadth of the mighty plain.

"Remain here," said Garth to his huntsmen. "Rest. Replenish your supplies of water. Gather your weapons. Summon the chieftains, woman—I shall take counsel with my brother, Tharn of Thandar, and will soon return." With those words he strode off across the camp in the direction of Tharn's tent, a kingly figure, straight as a soldier, his features clamped tight in a cold mask against the intolerable pain he bore in his heart.

Such was the dignity of the two High Chiefs that it would

have been unseemly had Tharn expressed his consternation at
the word that the daughter of Garth had been carried off by
beasts. Such men as they speak seldom, and to the point,
wasting neither words nor energy in displays of emotion.

They both knew exactly what was about to happen. The
two Cro-Magnon tribes, which had stood and fought together
shoulder to shoulder ever since the battle of the cavern-city
against the Gorpaks and the hideous Sluaggh, must now sun-
der their paths and go their separate ways—at least, for a
time.

It was, in fact, Tharn who suggested the inevitable.

"There is, in honor, no other way, my brother," he said
sternly. "During this long trek, you and your valiant warriors
have served me well in my own quest for my lost daughter,
Darya. It would be inconceivable for Tharn to ask that the
Omad Garth continue to assist him in his search, when now
the gomad Yualla has met with a similar fate. The tribes of
Sothar and of Thandar must now part. There is no other
course to follow."

"I agree," nodded Garth. "For blood calls to blood, and I
cannot stand idly by while at least a chance exists that my
child yet lives. Neither can I reasonably expect my brother
Tharn to abandon the search for his own child, to assist me
in my quest. We are agreed, then, that much as it grieves us
both—our paths must here part."

"It is agreed. We shall divide the stores and the weapons,
the garments and the tents and bedding, between us evenly,"
said Tharn. "Naught must be allowed to delay the departure
of the warriors of Sothar from the rescue."

"It may well be that we shall meet again," said the
Sotharian. "On his part, it is the wish of Garth the Omad
that such will prove the case. For, inasmuch as our own
homeland has been destroyed, the tribe of Sothar has
nowhere to go in a world filled with hostile tribes and enemies, both human and bestial. In such a world, my brother, it
is good to have found a friend."

The two men clasped each other's shoulder in the Zanthodonian equivalent of a hearty handshake.

And there was really nothing more to say.

The equal division of the supplies was swiftly accomplished, and farewells were made. During the time they had
marched and fought together, brief though it was, the men
and women and children of the two tribes had made many

friends, and partings are never pleasant. But time was of the essence, so the partings were brief.

While the men of Thandar stood silently watching, the tribe of Sotharians departed. There were no backward glances, and there were no tears. Fate had stepped between the two Cro-Magnon tribes, and that was all there was to it.

Garth struck out boldly into the midst of the plain, heading directly for the distant mountains which, as we know but he did not, formed a wall behind whose towering ramparts lay sheltered the Scarlet City of Zar.

With Sarga and his fleet-footed huntsmen in the lead to guide them, the tribe moved at a rapid pace. Both men and women could hold this steady pace for hours, if necessary, without yielding to fatigue. They are a hardy race, these direct descendants of our own Cro-Magnon ancestors, and virtually to the last individual they are superbly healthy physical specimens. I suppose this is because the life they lead is a hard one, with many perils, and thus the weak and sickly die early.

Garth did not know how distant the mountains were, for the Sotharians have not developed a system of measurements sophisticated enough to be of use. Neither did he have any notion of exactly how long it would take his tribe to reach the foothills of those mountains, because in their timeless world the Zanthodonians have no real conception of time.

He simply headed in the direction of his choice, knowing that he would eventually reach his goal.

As it chanced, other eyes were watching as the tribe traversed the grassy plains in search of the lost girl.

The people of Zar were effete, their vigor sapped by the endless round of pleasures, but they were not fools. The saying that the price of liberty is eternal vigilance would have struck a responsive chord within their breasts.

And the Dragon-riders who had captured the Professor and Xask and me were not the only mounted troops patrolling the plains which stretched before the gates of Zar.

Chapter 14

THE LANDSLIDE

The mighty wall of mountains which guarded the way to the Scarlet City was tall and sheer, but certainly not unscalable. The Cro-Magnon warriors took the climb by easy stages, resting often in order to conserve their strength. Only Hurok found the ascent truly difficult, but this was not because he lacked strength; no, it was that his bowed legs and splayed feet were not designed for mountaineering. However, he set his prognathous jaw grimly, and toiled along in the wake of the more lithe and limber Cro-Magnons.

Jorn the Hunter fell back in order to accompany his chieftain. A strange, almost unspoken comradeship had grown into being between the burly Neanderthal and the young huntsman. Neither could quite account for it, but it was there, nonetheless.

For an hour or so they climbed the sheer wall, finding hand- and foot-holds where you or I might have seen nothing. The vertigo which might well have claimed us did not bother them: true savages, children of the Dawn Age, they were as supple and fearless as monkeys, and could climb nearly as well.

How old these mountains might be none of them could tell, but the Professor has since voiced as his considered opinion that the Walls of Zar (as the denizens of the Scarlet City term this range) are relatively young. Doubtless they were thrust up from the bowels of the earth by volcanic forces in one of those titanic convulsions of nature which shaped our own world and that of Zanthodon. For the rock whereof they were composed was relatively soft and porous, and centuries of wind and rain had crumbled and flaked it into its present state. Ledges and crevices, wherein one might find temporary hand- and foot-holds, were numerous, which made the ascent of the sheer cliff vertiginous and laden with peril, but very far from impossible.

From time to time, the cliff was broken by a level ledge, where sheets of strata had crumbled or broken away. Seldom were these ledges more than a foot or two wide, but narrow as they were they afforded the warriors sufficient security to snatch a few moments rest before continuing the climb.

The goal for which they were striving was a cleft between the mountains which formed a pass. Unlike the dragon-guarded pass through which the Professor and I had been escorted by Captain Raphad and his Dragonmen, the pass to which Hurok and the others strove was situated much higher up the wall of the mountain. Still quite distant, it loomed above them tantalizingly. In time they would, of course, reach it, and from that point on the descent down the farther side should be much easier than the way up had proven to be.

Such, at least, was the hope of Hurok and the others.

It is to be regretted that Fate or Destiny, or whatever name you wish to use to designate the unseen and inscrutable Force which controls our lives, from time to time intervenes to frustrate our desires. The future is an unknown road veiled from our vision by clouds of mystery, and it is doubtless a great mercy that we are not permitted foreknowledge of those events which are yet to come, since there is no way known to men to avoid them.

Such was the case with Hurok and his men as they snatched a brief few moments of rest upon a narrow ledge. Suddenly, and without warning, that ledge and the mountainside wherefrom it obtruded, began to quiver as if to the beatings of a mighty heart. Small crumbs of rock, dislodged by the vibration, fell clattering down the cliff to sprinkle upon them as they crouched warily, eyes wide with alarm.

"The mountain shakes, O Hurok!" cried Varak. "What shall we do?"

The Apeman of Kor shook his head slowly. Nowhere within the reach of his eyes could he discern a cave opening or any other breach in the cliff wall wherein they might seek refuge from the hail of pebbles. And that this hail of pebbles might easily presage an avalanche was all too apparent to the Neanderthal.

Were a landslide to occur above their precarious perch, the tide of boulders resultantly dislodged would certainly sweep them from the ledge, hurtling them to a swift and sudden doom far below. And there was nothing which they could do to prevent this from happening, being men and not gods.

The warriors huddled upon the ledge peered about them fearfully. There was nowhere to go and naught that they could do. Whatever earthquake or volcanic perturbation might be the cause of the present danger, it was impossible to avoid the doom which yawned before them.

"Look!" cried Warza, suddenly pointing.

Hurok followed the direction in which his warrior was gesturing, and saw a portion of the cliff wall somewhat farther along the same ledge on which they crouched. At that point a massive outcropping of heavier, more weather-resistant ore thrust from the side of the cliff like a great sheltering hand. Were they to take refuge under that shelf of rock they might, just possibly, manage to avoid the rain of boulders which now they expected momentarily.

"Come—follow me!" boomed Hurok. Rising, and clinging to the quivering wall, he moved with slow and careful steps down the declination of the ledge and toward the spot where it seemed they might crouch in safety under the protection of the protruding shelf of stone. One by one, in single file, his warriors followed his example. They perforce ignored the pebbles and bits of stone which fell upon their heads and shoulders like hail; they squinted their eyes against the stinging clouds of rock dust which hissed and swirled about them.

And, far above their heads, they heard a mighty grinding, cracking, crunching sound, as of massive amounts of stone breaking loose from the upper peaks. . . .

Now that Yualla had found Murg, or vice versa, the two fell into argument concerning which route to take from this point on. Murg, as we already know, heartily craved the protection which would be afforded by his rejoining the host of the two tribes. But, as soon as he whiningly revealed that Hurok and Jorn and the others had launched an expedition to free Eric Carstairs and the Professor from the hands of Zar, the adventure-loving heart of the blonde girl desired to join in the excitement.

You must try to understand Yualla. Very seldom did the young spitfire manage to elude the stern and watchful gaze of her parents in order to enjoy an adventure of her own. Most of the time she was forced to submit patiently to being protected by those in whose care nature had placed her. Which did not mean that she submitted willingly, of course. . . .

But now that, through no fault of her own, she had perhaps only temporarily escaped from the vigilance of her father and his mate, the girl impulsively foresaw no
consequence more desirable than to seize the opportunity and
join the small band of warriors on their adventure.

She knew that her parents and friends would worry about
her. And she also knew that they probably feared her slain
and eaten by the pterodactyl. It was not that she intended to
inflict suffering upon those who loved her . . . it was just that
the temptation to play hooky for a little while was well nigh
irresistible.

Later, she would rejoin the tribe of Sothar, which would
rejoice at her return. And she, somewhat guiltily, was counting on that thankfulness which would well up within the
hearts of her family to forgive the small transgression which
she now considered.

"Yualla will journey to the mountains, to join with Hurok
and the other warriors," the girl said determinedly. "Murg,
however, may traverse the plain to rejoin the tribe of Sothar,
if such be the wish of Murg."

"Alone . . . ?" faltered the valiant Murg, lips dry, heart
pounding.

The cave-girl shrugged carelessly.

"If Murg wishes to rejoin the Sotharians, then he must
make his way back across the plains alone, for Yualla is determined to go forward toward the mountains," she said
firmly. "The decision is up to Murg."

Now, Murg all too clearly remembered the terrible encounter with the gigantic xunth, which had occurred on this very
plain and at no particular distance, too. And he also understood that the dreaded Dragonmen patrolled this grassland—
they who had seized and carried off Eric Carstairs and
Professor Potter. And, while Murg certainly did not want to
go back to face the scorn and contempt of the comrades he
had deserted and from whom he had thieved, the only alternative seemed even grimmer.

Having found companionship, Murg was exceedingly reluctant to abandon it.

So Murg at length yielded to Yualla's determination, and
began retracing his steps. Whining and whimpering every foot
of the way, he trudged gloomily along behind the briskly
striding girl toward the mountains.

It seemed to Murg, poor Murg, that the Fates were con-
spiring against him. Everytime he managed to escape from

one perilous situation, he was compelled to enter an even
more terrible one. It certainly wasn't fair, not fair at all!

All that long, interminable day, Murg slunk at the heels of
Yualla, until after many hours, weariness and hunger overcame the eager zestfulness of the high-spirited girl. Her bow
brought down game; a fire was built; they rested and fed,
lacking only a source of fresh water to appease their physical
needs.

The meal consumed, Yualla stretched out under the humid
skies of perpetual noon, closed her blue eyes, and promptly
fell asleep. Hers was the deep and undisturbed slumber of a
healthy young animal.

Murg, however, tossed and turned, unable to compose his
mind sufficiently to woo the slumbers which his weary and
aching muscles clamored.

From time to time, rolling over to seek a more comfortable
place amid the soft grasses, the little man glanced accusingly
over to where the girl lay sound asleep. Nor did the rise and
fall of her firm pointed breasts elude the lingering gaze of
Murg, nor the sleek length of her bare thighs and slender
legs.

It was then that an alternative to following Yualla's path
occurred to Murg. If the girl could be bound, made subject to
his will, helpless to oppose his slightest whim, he could go
where he pleased without giving up the pleasures of companionship in peril.

His eyes lingering on the slim body of the half-naked girl,
it came into the mind of Murg that those companionable
pleasures, in the present instance, might well prove headier
and more exciting than had heretofore entered into his imagination. . . .

Eyes gloating on the nude flesh of the girl, a cunning smile
creasing his thin lips, Murg chuckled throatily, and began to
creep toward the sleeping girl across the grasses. . . .

Chapter 15

THE LIPS OF ZARYS

When Ialys, the Empress's handmaiden, led me from the banqueting hall for what she had euphemistically described as "a private audience," I felt a sinking sensation in the pit of my stomach. I had a nasty hunch the audience was going to be a lot more than just "private"—*intimate*, would be more like it.

The only thing that pleased me about the prospect was the venomous glance of purest hate Cromus shot after me as he watched me leave. I had the feeling that splendid fellow had designs in that direction, himself . . . and why not? What better way for an unscrupulous, ambitious officer to gain the coveted crown than by wooing and winning the beautiful young woman who currently wore the royal bauble?

Not that the Divine Zarys was not worthy of being coveted completely for herself, with or without a crown. She was, truly, one of the most exquisite women I have ever had the good luck to set eyes upon. . . .

This being the case, my reader may legitimately wonder why I felt so squeamish about the amorous tussle which I anticipated in the immediate offing. I spent a few moments rather pondering the same question, myself. After all, I have spent a lot of years knocking around some of the seamier corners of the world, and more than a few lovely ladies have succumbed to my raffish charm. I have never exactly taken vows of chastity, either. Why, then, did I more or less dread the coming "interview"?

I guess it's because, being an old-fashioned man in some ways, I like to be the one that makes the passes. To be summoned into the royal bedchamber gets my back up; not that it has ever happened before, of course. It's rather like being sent for as one sends for a pet dog.

And I don't intend to be anyone's lapdog.

Ialys led me into a high, vaulted chamber whose walls
were of fretted alabaster through which a lustrous, dim light
shone softly, transforming the interior of the circular room
into something which I imagine is very like the heart of a
hollow pearl.

Glowing fruits in bowls of hammered silver rested on low
tabourets of rare woods. Wine breathed from an open am-
phora which sat in a bed of crushed ice. The floor, tiled entirely in three kinds of jade, was covered—not by carpeting,
but by silken furs. Ornaments and fixtures glittered with cut
jewels. The room breathed luxury from every pore: only un-
limited power and unimaginable wealth could have fashioned
such a nest.

In the center of the chamber lay a sort of chaise longue
draped with gleaming fabrics, and heaped with many small,
plump cushions colored magenta, orange, canary, lavender,
and pink.

Thereon reposed the Empress. Her long-sleeved feasting
gown had been discarded in favor of a voluminous and very
transparent peignoir of fragile lace. Beneath this flimsy robe
her tender flesh was bare: warm, naked womanflesh gleamed
through the interstices of the woven lace.

At the foot of this couch Ialys left me, with a single, demure smiling glance. I felt very foolish and awkward just
standing there, but there was nowhere for me to sit, unless I
wished to share the Empress's couch. And that was coming
soon enough, I thought uncomfortably.

She selected a ripe grape from a bowl near the chaise longue
and popped the morsel of fruit between soft, rosy lips.
All the while she looked me over with a slow, appraising
glance that was thoughtful, even admiring, but somehow not
degrading.

"It is customary, Eric Carstairs," she said after a moment,
"for lesser mortals to prostrate themselves in my presence."

I opened my mouth to say something inane, or stubborn,
or possibly both; but she stilled me with a lazy gesture.

"However, I sense that you are not the sort of man who
willingly prostrates himself, even before goddesses," she observed with a slight smile.

I grinned back.

"As a matter of fact, Majesty, I'm not."

"Your candor is refreshing to ears soothed by flattery and

lies," she said. "However, I could always have you beaten to your knees, as Cromus attempted earlier. . . ."

"Yes, you could," I acknowledged.

We studied each other for a time. Then:

"I do not intend to do so," she remarked, "for men such as you I suspect to be rare. Let us speak frankly together, Eric Carstairs, setting aside for the time the contest of wills. I have need of men such as you—"

"Frankly, I speak a lot better when I'm sitting down," I said, interrupting. For a long instant I thought I had gone too far, for her magnificent eyes flashed with imperious fury and her superb bosom heaved tumultuously. Then she calmed: her self-control was extraordinary for a personage who seldom if ever is required to use self-control.

"You *dare*—!"

I shrugged. In for a penny, in for a pound.

"If you want a man to grovel and whine at your feet," I pointed out, "you have a banquet hall full of them back there. I thought you were looking for another sort of man."

She threw back her head and uttered a peal of silvery laughter. Then, with a sinuous movement, she curled up like a kitten at one end of the chaise longue and patted the other with the tips of her fingers.

"Sit, then, Eric Carstairs, if it will serve the better to loosen your tongue."

I sat down. I accepted a goblet of wine. I drank thirstily. And all the while she studied me, darting oblique little glances at me from under the shadowings of her sooty lashes.

"You interest me, Eric Carstairs . . . you are very unlike the other men that I have known hitherto. They are either cringing and cowardly, or greedy and self-serving, or direct and brutal."

"Like Cromus," I said.

"Like Cromus," she agreed with a smile. "How you pleased me when you felled him with your bare hands! It is a remarkable art; some time you must demonstrate it for me again."

"The next time somebody tries to push me around, I'll do just that," I promised.

"You are direct, but honest," she observed. "Self-serving, I suspect, but uncompromising. Capable of brutal actions, but able to be gentle, as I also suspect."

I said nothing, flushing just a little, which, in the dim nacreous light, probably wasn't visible. It made me less than comfortable to be praised to my face; but, then, I'm not exactly sure I was being praised, come to think of it.

"You are a barbarian, for all men of Zanthodon that are not the men of Zar are barbarians. But your culture and breeding are as obvious as are your physical attributes. Tell me, Eric Carstairs: the country from which you come, is it very distant from my kingdom?"

"It's quite a ways away," I admitted. Which was only the honest truth, as the good old U.S.A. was a couple of hundred miles straight up and on the other side of the globe from this subterranean world under the Sahara.

"And are all of the men in your country very much like yourself?"

"Well, some are and some aren't. But there's an awful lot of them that are."

"It must be an interesting country, then. And . . . are the women of your homeland as beautiful as am I?"

"Very, very few of them," I answered with complete and utter honesty.

That pleased her! She smiled a lazy, languorous smile.

"And is there a woman of your country who awaits your return . . . a mate, perhaps?"

"There is not."

"But when you first saw me, there enthroned in the Pasiphaeum, you seemed to know me at one look. And I read many emotions in your face . . ."

I colored a little.

"There is a young woman of the tribes," I explained, "to whom Your Majesty bears a strange resemblance . . ."

"Indeed?" She wrinkled up her pert little nose fastidiously. "How odd! And you—love this young woman of the tribes?"

Something cautioned me to tread carefully here. So I temporized just a little.

"Well . . . she and I barely know each other . . . and we have been very long apart from each other," I said at last.

It seemed to have been the sort of answer that Zarys wanted to hear, for a flash of satisfaction gleamed and was gone in her lustrous eyes. She relaxed with another of those lazy, catlike movements, and laid her hand upon my arm almost caressingly.

"You are strong," she murmured softly, "so strong . . . and I have been so long among fools and weaklings . . . with a man such as yourself at my side, what an empire I could carve from this savage world!"

Here it comes, I thought grimly to myself.

Quite suddenly she was in my arms, her own slim arms twined about my neck, her panting breasts bare against my chest, and the sweetness of her perfume heady and intoxicating in my nostrils.

But her lips were even sweeter. . . .

She broke off the kiss, gasping for breath. I felt dizzy and half-drunk, torn between arousal and disgust.

As she uncoiled from my embrace, she struck something from the tabouret at her side. It had been covered by a silken scarf. It fell to the tiled floor with a clang.

I looked down and saw my .45 automatic.

Part Four

———◆———

THE
DIVINE
ZARYS

Chapter 16

LEAP FOR LIFE

As Hurok and his warriors sought safety beneath the sheltering crag above the ledge, the mountain shook and huge fragments of stone were torn loose and began to thunder down the mountainside in an avalanche.

It was indescribably horrible to look up and see great, jagged boulders hurtling directly toward you. What made the experience all the more terrible was that there was hardly anything you could do to protect yourself from the spinning rocks as they bounced and slid and fell toward the narrow little ledge in a massive and deadly rain.

As the ledge was too narrow to afford passage to men except in single file, one of the warriors had, of necessity, to be the last in line. And, as it happened, this was Jorn the Hunter. Already the landslide had very nearly reached the ledge, and Jorn knew that he could not reach the shelter of that rocky shelf which jutted out above the ledge in time to take refuge beneath it.

There was truly nothing to do—but jump.

The urge for self-preservation is strong within the hearts of all men. But it is perhaps strongest within the breast of a savage warrior such as young Jorn. Even though to leap from the ledge was suicidal, it was the only action which the young Cro-Magnon could conceivably take. For the alternative was simply to stand there and dumbly wait for the landslide to sweep him to a gory death. And any action, however hopeless, was preferable to *that*.

Jorn sprang from the ledge and fell as fell the heavy stones above him. He vanished from the sight of his comrades in an instant.

As Jorn vanished, Hurok uttered an inarticulate cry: it was a roar of bestial rage and loss, quickly stifled. The other warriors who clung together under the sheltering slab said nothing, their faces drawn and grim. The loss of a comrade was a common enough occurrence in their primitive existence. But Jorn had made good friends, and all in their number liked the youth.

The avalanche swept down about them in deafening thunder. Whirling clouds of bitter rock dust enveloped them. Fragments and splinters of stone pelted them. The ledge shuddered beneath where they crouched. Darkness closed upon them. The shelf of stone above their heads groaned to the impact of the landslide—which parted to either side of the projecting slab as a spur of rock parts asunder a waterfall.

The air cleared; the thunder died in the distance below.

No longer did the mountain shiver to the impulse of hidden volcanic forces.

One by one they emerged from the shelter of the slab, coated with gray dust, shaken and bruised, but otherwise unharmed.

No word was spoken regarding the loss of Jorn the Hunter, for there was nothing to say.

Looking above him, Hurok of Kor saw that the landslide had cracked and scored and pitted the surface of the cliff overhead. The climb, from this point on, would be swifter and easier than it had been before.

Grunting a command, he reached up, grabbed the projecting rock which had saved them from certain death, and hoisted himself upon it.

They began to climb.

Garth and the tribe of Sothar marched across the plains in the direction in which the thakdol had borne away his daughter, Yualla.

The scouts and huntsmen of the Sotharians ranged far afield, searching for any sign or token that the young girl was dead or alive. With keen eyes, alert and vigilant, they scanned the thick grasses, the muddy places, the many small, meandering streams, but without finding that which they sought.

It seemed dreadfully likely to the chieftains of Garth's council that the thakdol had carried Yualla home to its nest, to feed its young upon her flesh. This was, after all, the way of hunting thakdols from time immemorial, and there occurred to them no reason why a thakdol should change its habits now.

A realistic man—for monarchs should be practical, at very least—Garth inwardly agreed with the assessment of his counselors as to the gomad Yualla's grisly fate. But within his mighty breast there lurked an optimist, as well; and he determined that he would not give over the quest until positive proof had been found, or until such time had elapsed that the last faint hope of his daughter's survival dwindled and died.

As they marched, they hunted and slew game. When they made their brief camps to rest and refresh themselves, the women of the tribe cooked the game thus taken, and they fed.

These pauses to rest were, as I have said, brief, for time was of the essence—an apparent contradiction in a people innocent of the very concept of time, I know, but I can do no other than record here what they did without trying to interpret what I cannot understand or explain.

Suffice it to say, some inward urge—call it an instinct of necessity—drove them constantly on, and they paused to rest only when they must. In a world without beasts to ride, where the remotest ancestor of the horse is a small plump mammal no bigger than a collie, men must perforce travel on what used to be called shank's mare. They must walk.

With every waking period of the march, the barrier of mountains known as the Walls of Zar crept nearer. After every sleep, they arose to find the mountains before them still tantalizingly distant, but no more distant than the "night" before.

And somewhere among those fang-like peaks, in an untidy nest littered with thakdol droppings, might repose the gnawed bones of young Yualla.

Conversely, somewhere amid that wilderness of jagged and cloven rock, she might well be wandering—lost, alone, hungry and defenseless, having by some miracle survived the claws and fangs of the pterodactyl.

It was that hope which drove them on.

Unfortunately for the warriors of Sothar, the people of the Scarlet City did not depend upon the mountainous barrier alone to protect them from the savage tribes and monsters which shared this world with them.

For these plains were patrolled by the Dragonmen, that guard of Zarian males who rode mounted on great, stalking dinosaurs tamed by the mysterious telepathic crystals which the wizards of Zàr had long ages ago perfected.

They were not numerous, these patrols, but numbers are not needed when you ride upon the backs of monster reptiles thirty feet in length. They tended to follow no fixed patrol routes, but to trace huge, random circles before the walls of Zar. And on one of these circuitous rides, the Dragonmen espied—still a great way off, but steadily coming nearer—the Sotharian host.

As things turned out, it was the squadron of Captain Raphad which discovered the approach of the Sotharians. This same officer, you will recall, had been responsible for the capture of Xask, Professor Potter, and myself, although there is a considerable difference between seizing two or three men, and facing a pitched battle against hundreds of stout warriors.

Whereas the folk of Zar, the city-dwellers, sheltering behind that mighty range of mountains, guarded from harm by their vigilant patrols of Dragonmen, tended to dismiss the Cro-Magnon tribes as mere ignorant, naked, superstitious savages—Raphad knew better. He had faced and fought the blond barbarians before, and he knew and respected their fighting prowess and dauntless courage.

While the Cro-Magnon warriors were fighting men of superb skill and bravery, the one thing they lacked, to Raphad's way of thinking, was discipline. Like all savages, the Cro-Magnon tribesmen fought individually, chieftains taking a stand surrounded by their own warriors, rather than presenting a united front as was the custom among civilized nations such as the ancient Minoan colony.

Raphad clambered up the long neck to the head of his reptilian mount, and from that lofty vantage point scanned the approaching host. He could not count individuals from such a distance, but it was obvious to him that the Cro-Magnons were to be numbered in the hundreds.

While many of these would be women and children, of course, this did little to lessen the advantage in numbers which the strangers held over his squadron. For the blond savages are taught the cruel arts of survival from their mothers' breasts, and even the women and older children make dangerous and formidable adversaries in an open conflict.

As ever, Raphad counted upon the fear which his monster saurians inspired in the breasts of the barbarians to weigh mightily in his favor. Always, on previous encounters, had this proven greatly to his advantage, and doubtless it would do so now.

For the mighty dinosaurs are the most fearsome and enormous brutes the world has ever known, and the Cro-Magnon and Neanderthal warriors give them wide berth, avoiding them if at all possible. This is only common sense, when you find yourself face to face with something weighing many tons.

Of course, the giant lizards upon which Captain Raphad and his scouts were mounted were not meat-eating predators, but were instead docile and relatively harmless vegetarians. But the Cro-Magnons rarely had the leisure to differentiate between the meat-eaters and the grass-eaters, preferring to avoid anything taller than the trees.

And even a placid vegetarian the size of a two-story house can tread men to slime underfoot. . . .

Therefore, without particular trepidation, Raphad ordered his men forward so as to meet the Sotharians face to face.

Even as Raphad spied from afar the Sotharians, so of course did the Sotharians spy from afar the Zarians. In fact, they saw the Dragonmen first, mounted, as they were, on the monstrous reptiles.

Garth of Sothar set his jaw grimly. That these were foemen was certain: in his savage world, all strangers are considered enemies, until proven otherwise.

And he greatly feared the huge lumbering brutes upon which the slender olive-skinned men were so curiously mounted, and which they had so mysteriously under their control.

Nevertheless, he drew up his men for battle, positioning the women and children in the rear with the baggage. His fighting chieftains each sought advantage of the best ground possible—a knoll or hillock, or a hedgy place of concealment, with their warriors ranged about them, shields of tanned hide sheltering their bodies, spears and axes and bows at the ready.

As there seemed to be no way to avoid the encounter, then let it come: that was Garth's fatalistic philosophy.

He stood, massive arms folded upon his mighty chest, and watched the line of Dragonmen approach with slow and ponderous tread. . . .

Chapter 17

WHEN ZARYS COMMANDS

There was no question about it—it was my pistol. There could not possibly be two Colt .45's here in the Underground World!

Which meant that Xask—that wily schemer!—had gotten to the Empress at some point, and had told her of the power of my "thunder-weapon," as the Zanthodonians called it. This meant that all of the other tribes and nations of Zanthodon were in mighty big trouble. For Zarys would not have been Zarys had she not lusted to extend her empire to cover as much of the subterranean world as could be conquered.

"You recognize the weapon, do you not?" Zarys demanded, with one of those lightning changes of mood that I was to discover part of her mercurial makeup. I acknowledged the fact, as there was nothing to be gained by a pretense of ignorance.

"And is it truly as terrible as Xask has described?" she pressed.

"Terrible enough," I admitted.

"And did he truly slay a gigantic drunth with your thunder-weapon?" she inquired sharply.

I shrugged. "As to that, Majesty, I cannot say, for I did not see him do it." Which was only the honest truth, after all.

"Xask has told me of the drunth he slew with a single stroke of lightning from your device," she said.*

Now, a drunth is quite a hefty critter, to be sure. Professor Potter believes it to be the same as the stegosaurus, and it's bigger than a fire engine. So if Xask really did fell a drunth with a single shot, it must have been pure and simple luck.

* Xask actually did shoot a drunth and kill it with a single bullet. See Chapter 20 of *Zanthodon*, the second volume of the memoirs of Eric Carstairs.

And I said as much to Zarys.

She seemed satisfied, purring with pleasure, fondling the automatic sensuously. I would have snatched it from her if I had dared, but something in the demure glance she gave me told me that guards were positioned nearby—behind the wall-hangings, perhaps, or in niches behind that screen of carved and lacy alabaster.

For one moment I thought of taking the gun and holding Zarys as a hostage, forcing her to permit our escape from the city. But where, in the winding and labyrinthine ways of the Scarlet City was the Professor right now—for I certainly could not leave without him.

No, this was not the time to try for an escape. There were too many things I needed to know, like how to get out of the city, for instance, and how to get across the mountains. So I held off, if only for a while, cursing my faint-heartedness.

This opportunity might never come again, I grimly knew.

Zarys touched a chime. A single bell-like note rang sweetly. The handmaiden, Ialys, entered and knelt by the couch to touch her brows against the bare feet of her Empress.

Zarys indicated the automatic.

"Show me," she said.

I blinked, astounded.

"How—?"

She nudged Ialys with the toes of one rosy foot.

"Kill this slave," she said, not even glancing down at the girl who knelt on the furs of the floor.

I set my jaw truculently.

"I don't murder people in cold blood," I snapped. "Especially not people who have never harmed me!"

Temper flared in her magnificent eyes.

"When Zarys commands, lesser mortals obey!"

"Not *this* lesser mortal, lady," I growled. From her kneeling position at the Empress's feet, Ialys shot me one unreadable glance in which astonishment, gratitude, and some third emotion were mingled.

Her superb breasts heaving with the tumult of her emotions, the Empress stared at me as if trying to conquer my will by her will alone. I matched her stare for stare, though inwardly I had some qualms about getting out of this spot with a whole skin.

Then her mood changed again, and she became playful.

"If I summon Xask, will you demonstrate your weapon upon *him?*" she demanded with a faint smile.

Well, I was tempted. I admit it. Xask was certainly no friend of mine; in fact, I owed him a couple right in the chops. On the other hand, what I had already said was perfectly true. I will kill an enemy in combat any way I can, sure. I will kill to save a friend, of course. I will kill to protect a woman, beyond question. But I have never in my. life murdered anybody in cold blood, and I didn't intend to start here.

Certainly not just to impress a painted temptress like Zarys of Zar. . . .

I shook my head. Whether or not the gesture is understood in the Scarlet City, she must have been able to read the answer in my face.

She tapped her fingers on the carven arm of the couch, studying me meditatively.

"I could have you whipped, or beaten," she remarked.

"So you could," I growled.

"Why are you so stubborn?"

I had to laugh, although it came out more like a snarl.

"A few minutes ago you were praising me for being uncompromising," I reminded her. "Now you want to whip me for being uncompromising. Doesn't make much sense to me!"

She must have agreed with me, in spite of herself, for a mischievous twinkle shone in the depths of her eyes, and the corners of her lips twitched in a brief half-smile.

"Well . . . we shall discuss these and other matters further, at a later time," drawled the Empress lazily, stretching like a cat and putting away the automatic—very carefully, I noticed.

Ialys rose to her feet and led me from the chamber that was like a hollowed pearl.

I was almost trembling with exhaustion from that interview, but somehow I had gotten away with it.

Maybe the Divine Zarys rather liked to be faced up to and denied something . . . after all, it must have been a novel experience for her!

At first, Jorn fell like a stone, turning end over end. The speed of his descent was such that the wind tore the breath from his lungs, and the boy knew that long before he could be hurtled to death against the rocky floor beneath he would likely perish of suffocation.

To hurl from a height to dash your brains out against

jagged rocks is a cruel death, to be sure. But to die as young as Jorn the Hunter, with most of your life still ahead of you in the womb of the unborn future, is doubly cruel. . . .

The wind whipped his eyes savagely, making them water. Squinting against the gale, Jorn suddenly spied the glimmer of a mysterious blueness beneath him, as the floor of the plain came rushing up toward him—

Then the sheer instinct for survival took over.

He extended his legs behind him, pressing them together. He pointed his arms over his head, hands pressed palm to palm. And what had been a whirling fall turned into a perfect dive.

Cold water struck him a numbing blow. He cleaved the surface, stunned from the impact, and touched the muddy bottom of the little mountain lake that had broken his fall.

The icy shock of the water about him roused him from his state of momentary unconsciousness. Kicking against the lake bottom, he floundered clumsily back to the surface again.

All about him, heavy boulders fell, churning the surface of the lake into exploding froth.

Sucking air into starved lungs, he dove again, and swam toward the nearest shore. To every side, rocks sank through the muddy water. One grazed his shoulder, another scraped against his leg. But luckily, the impact of striking the lake surface had broken the fall of the rocks as it had broken his, and they sank through the water too slowly for these collisions to do him any particular harm.

He dragged himself out upon a rocky shelf and lay there, gasping for breath.

He felt pummeled and bruised, and he ached in every muscle known to anatomy. Groggy, shaken, bone-weary—yet, miraculously, he still lived!

After a brief rest, Jorn felt much recovered from his narrow scrape with doom.

The hot, humid air of Zanthodon dried his flesh and warmed the chill from his bones. He had taken no injury from his fall into the lake, although a split second one way or another and the impact could easily have snapped his spine or broken his legs.

Fortune seemed to be smiling upon Jorn the Hunter.

When he felt better enough to move, the boy looked around, taking stock of his situation.

All of his weapons had been lost in the fall; he retained

nothing of his accouterments but the scrap of fur wound
about his loins, the thong which bound the loin-covering to
his lean waist, and his sandals.

Above him, lifted the mountain. Jorn groaned within him
at the thought of attempting to climb that height again, especially in his present bruised and shaken condition. Food
would do much to restore him to his full strength and alertness, but where could he find anything to kill, here in this
rocky wilderness among the foothills?

He headed out upon the grassy plains, having found a
sharp splinter of rock, hoping to make a lucky kill.

Instead, he saw someone who was about the last person in
all the world whom he could have expected to see. . . .

Chapter 18

THE CUNNING OF XASK

One moment Yualla was sound asleep, deep in the innocent slumbers of the young and healthy—the next instant she
was shocked awake. To find herself crushed under the panting weight of Murg!

The scrawny little man writhed atop her, striving with one
hand to pin her wrists above her head while with his other
hand he fumbled, pawing at her naked breasts, with his hot
breath searing her face as his slobbering lips sought her
mouth.

The girl was frightened, and amazed. Rape was not a
crime unknown to her primitive society, but it was a rare
one, truly. The tribe of Sothar was small and inbred so that
nearly every male was related, however distantly, to nearly
every female—cousins, second and third cousins, and so on.
And in nearly every society known to man, incest has been
the most loathsome and despicable of crimes.

Yualla, however, remained frozen by shock and surprise
for moments only. The gasping, grunting creature which
wriggled atop her, clawing at the brief garment about her
loins, was thin and scrawny. And he was no fighting man,
was Murg. So—

Writhing to one side, turning her head away from Murg's
foul-breathed kisses, the lithe jungle girl raised one leg sharply between the legs of her assailant. Her smoothly muscled
thigh caught him a shrewd blow in the crotch—and, in the
same instant, her pointed elbow struck the little man in the
breast, just below the heart, where a cluster of ganglia lie
which are extremely sensitive.

Murg voiced a strangled yelp. His face turned the un-
wholesome hue of dirty milk. Gagging and retching, he fell
aside, clutching himself and moaning in sick pain. For a time
he was unable to do aught else but roll about the grassy

ground, grasping at his injured parts and groaning at the well-nigh intolerable pain.

Erelong, when he was sufficiently recovered from the girl's blows to become cognizant of his surroundings once again, he peered up to see Yualla standing alertly near, her clear eyes fierce with cold fury, her lovely features hard and grim. And in her tanned, capable hands she held her hunting bow, a long arrow nocked and pointed unwaveringly at his heart.

"M-mercy, my Princess!" he babbled, thoroughly frightened and fearing his death was impending. "Forgive poor, crazed Murg, whom your beauty has driven mad—but only for a moment!" he added hastily, as the thought struck him that the jungle girl might well decide to put him out of his misery if she truly believed him crazed.

"Murg knew very well what he was attempting to do," said the girl in level tones, eyes hard and unforgiving. "And Murg knows very well what Yualla's sire, the mighty Garth, would do to him in punishment for his daring to put his dirty paws upon the person of the gomad of Sothar—"

Murg thought about that for a moment, remembering the burly shoulders and deep chest and massive thews of the High Chief. And he licked dry lips uneasily, shuddering at the thought of the terrible vengeance Garth would extract from his hide.

"Do not kill poor Murg," he babbled fearfully. "Make him your slave, merciful lady, to fetch and carry for you, to toil and labor, and to fight valiantly in your behalf. . . ."

At that, Yualla had trouble repressing a smile. The very thought of Murg, that whining and treacherous little coward, doing anything in a fight besides trying to run away from it, brought the element of humor into the situation.

"Very well, perhaps, after all, Yualla will permit the miserable Murg to live a little longer," the girl said, beginning to relent a little. "Turn over on your face and put your hands together behind your back."

"The beautiful Princess would not slay poor old Murg from behind, surely?" whimpered the little man cautiously.

She shook her head, blond mane tousling about bare, tanned shoulders. "Not I; but Yualla can hardly trust Murg unless his hands are bound. Now, do as I say, or we shall end this matter here and now, and the grass of the plains will drink the thin, weak blood of the cowardly Murg!"

Hastily, Murg rolled over and pressed his face into the meadow grass, while Yualla knelt and bound his wrists together in the small of his back, using a spare bowstring in lieu of a rope of woven grass. Then she kicked him to his feet.

"Now we shall continue on our way, as Yualla no longer feels the need of sleep, and the quicker we traverse the distance between this place and the mountains, the sooner we shall join the warriors of Sothar and Thandar who search for Eric Carstairs," she said.

And without further speech, she set off over the plain, in rapid, long-legged stride, without looking back. The unhappy Murg must perforce scramble to his feet and trot along after her; nor did he dare whine or complain about the pace which she had set. For were she to abandon him here like this, bound and helpless and without any weapon, he would fall prey to the first monstrous predator who came his way.

Speaking of Murg reminds me of that other wily and cunning traitor, Xask, former vizier of Kor and exile of the Scarlet City. The differences between the two men are only a matter of degree, save that Xask was far more clever than Murg, and less tempted by lust, and certainly no coward.

Both Xask and Murg were driven by self-interest, but Xask was willing to take great risks to attain the power he sought, while Murg simply hungered for a safe, snug life without danger. To have placed himself once again within the power of Zar was a hazardous and dangerous risk, but it was one which Xask had gladly taken, for the stakes were high. No sooner had he been brought within the palace-citadel which crowned the heights of the island-city, than Xask sought a private audience with the Empress who had condemned him to outlawry and exile. Curious as to what had impelled him to return to the kingdom which he was forbidden to enter upon pain of execution, Zarys permitted the interview.

She listened dubiously to his fantastic account of the powers of the thunder-weapon, and, with great skepticism, to his protestations of loyalty. Women such as Zarys are not likely to be taken in by men such as Xask, and the two thoroughly understood one another. It did not seem to Zarys that Xask could possibly be lying about the titanic power of the weapon, for his claim could swiftly be exposed as a lie by a simple demonstration. Therefore, his claims as to its effectiveness must, after all, be true, no matter how fantastic they might sound.

Zarys knew exactly what Xask hoped to gain by delivering

the secret of the thunder-weapon into her hands: he hoped to regain in full the power and authority which he had lost when his plots against her throne had been exposed. Having enjoyed the ultimate in power since she was a child, Zarys knew very well what a heady intoxicant it was, and she was more than willing to restore Xask to his former position of influence if he could, indeed, render up the secret of the weapon.

Power and authority and influence with the throne—these are the payments whereby queens purchase the service of intelligent and gifted men. But this time, Zarys determined to keep a careful watch on Xask. There would be no more plots against her, not a second time.

The two understood each other perfectly. Xask, given the freedom of the palace, wasted no time in seeking out the sumptuous apartments where Professor Potter and Eric Carstairs had been lodged. He found only the Professor in residence, for I was then awaiting my own private audience with Her Nibs.

The scrawny scientist was reclining blissfully on a couch strewn with silken stuffs, nibbling on grapes, while giggling slave girls trimmed and perfumed his stiff little spike of snowy beard and the wisps which fringed his balding dome, buffed his fingernails, and shaved his lean, bestubbled cheeks. Professor Potter seemed to be enjoying himself hugely; but, then, after weeks and months spent tramping through the jungles, crawling through noisome caverns, sloshing about in swamps, and otherwise enduring the discomforts of the wilderness life, why shouldn't a few of the amenities of civilization have pleased him?

Xask wasted no time in getting directly to the point. The wily Zarian knew almost by instinct when to be threatening, when to be conciliatory, and when to appeal to reason. On this occasion, he assumed the outward trappings of complete honesty, somewhat leavened with urgency and directness.

"I know that you and your friend dislike me and distrust me," he began, for he could read the older man's suspicions in the distrustful gaze with which the Professor examined him. "And, in all truth, my friend, we have been at odds in the past. Now, however, our interests coincide, and I must admit to a certain guiltiness. It is not impossible that, had I not interfered with you and Eric Carstairs, neither of you would presently find yourselves immured in this silken dungeon."

"I am glad to hear you have the honesty to admit to your treacheries," sniffed the Professor. "But I have no reason to presume that the leopard has changed his spots—oh, you know what I mean!—and I warn you, my friend, that you will not find Percival P. Potter, Ph.D., as easy to befool as you found Fumio and One-Eye—!"

"I am certain of that," said Xask, his beautiful orator's voice ringing with sincerity. "For I well know that, in your native land, wherever that may be, you are recognized as a great savant, revered for his wisdom and his scholarly attainments."

I suppose the Professor would not have been completely human had he not relaxed a little at this point, basking in praise which, to be frank, he believed honestly earned. Xask pressed on, sensing his momentary advantage.

"It was, as you know, my intention to obtain from yourself and your fine young friend the secrets of the thunder-weapon so as to present them before the throne of the Divine Zarys," he said. "What you do not, however, realize, is my reason for wishing to obtain those secrets. You will have assumed, I am afraid, that it was simple greed and the cold ambition which leads to the lust for power."

"Well, ah, to be honest. . . ."

"Nothing could be further from the truth!" declared Xask. "I am a patriot, sir! My one desire is to serve my Empress, and my fellow countrymen, and to preserve them from danger and destruction, inasmuch as it is within my power to do so. Here you see a dying people of dwindling power who have attained to the superior heights of urban civilization, although ringed about with savages and terrible beasts. The warlike spirit of our conquering ancestors has long ago deserted us; our legions weaken, not only in numbers but in morale and fighting skills. It is the thunder-weapon and the thunder-weapon alone which may sustain us in a hostile and savage world."

"Um," said the Professor.

"I assume that the level of your civilization is superior to our own," said Xask cunningly. "For to invent such a device as the thunder-weapon presupposes an advanced culture of great artisans and scholars and philosophers. But I somehow feel inwardly convinced that your people are only more advanced in *degree* above my own, and that we are not all that terribly far behind you: tell me, sir, am I not close to the truth?"

Professor Potter licked his lips, thinking of New Crete which, with its flush toilets and hot and cold running water, was a considerably higher civilization than certain rural towns in Mississippi and Alabama which he had visited, and which lacked these same amenities to a noticeable degree.

"Well, ah, to tell the truth," he muttered lamely.

Xask smiled. The elderly outlander might be more learned than he in strange skills and curious lore, but he was as easily coerced as any other human mortal whom Xask had yet encountered.

Then he told the Professor what he wanted him to do.

Chapter 19

THE HUNTER
AND THE HUNTED

Garth watched grimly as the half-circle of Zarian guards approached the place where his host had taken its stand. He did not fear the olive-hued, strangely clothed little men, for they were few in numbers, slim and short of build, lightly armed. What he *did* fear was the tremendous beasts they rode, which he knew as thodars; Professor Potter might have identified them as a subspecies of brontosaurus, smaller and lighter than a true brontosaurus, and adapted to life on the plains rather than in the swamps and marshes, but still formidable and mighty beasts, with their long, snaky necks, barrel bodies, and long tapering tails.

They were coated in a slick, leathery hide a dark greenish-gray in coloration, paling to yellowish-white on the underside and belly. They moved along on huge, bowed legs as thick around as tree trunks, ending in splayed feet whose ponderous tread shook the earth. They must have weighed tons, and brave indeed would be the warrior willing to face them in battle.

The psychological advantage of taming and riding the great thodars was an obvious one. Professor Potter, had he been present to watch the effect these ponderous, lumbering reptiles had on the brave and stalwart Cro-Magnon fighting men, might well have been reminded of the devastating psychological impact which the ancient Greeks and Romans suffered every time they faced in battle Eastern armies mounted on Indian elephants. The only difference here was that the thodars were at least five times the size and weight of the largest Indian elephant ever seen.

The small Zarian with the gilded cuirass who rode the lead thodar and who was probably Captain Raphad, as his brows

were crowned with the orichalcum band which bore the tele-
phathic crystal which controlled the giant brutes, uttered a
shrill command in a language hitherto unheard by the men of
Sothar. At once, and in perfect order, the riders urged their
beasts into something which resembled a charge in slow motion.

The ground literally trembled under the mighty feet of the
advancing circle of thodars. Warrior of Sothar glanced at
warrior of Sothar; men paled, licked lips suddenly dry, but no
one broke and ran.

"We do not stand a chance, my Omad," said one of
Garth's chieftains who stood near. No fear was audible in his
quiet tones, only a somber hopelessness.

Garth considered, frowning. Behind his majestic brows, his
alert and agile mind raced. For what the chieftain had said
was perfectly true: there was no hope of slaying beasts so
mighty as these. Bristling with a score of spears, they would
still remain on their feet and moving forward.

Suddenly, out of nowhere, inspiration struck. Garth, although a primitive Cro-Magnon savage, was a great leader of
men in peace and in war; and great leaders have at least one
thing in common, that being the ability to devise bold new
methods of warfare. Alexander, Napoleon, Caesar, Hannibal,
all have possessed this uncanny knack, and triumphed over
incredible numbers. Which is why we remember them as
great leaders, rather than the foes, like Vercingetorix and
Darius, whom they soundly defeated!

"Bowmen! *Pick off the riders!* Do not attempt to slay the
thodars, nor even to injure them!" he cried in a great voice
like a roll of thunder.

The wisdom of Garth's words instantly struck new courage
and fortitude into the hearts of his wavering men. All knew
the thodars to be placid and docile grass-eaters rather than
dangerous carnivores. With their riders slain, the beasts might
very well wander off to crop the meadow grasses, indifferent
to the presence of the Sotharians.

Bows were strung and lifted, feathered bows were bent until featured tips touched the earlobes of the archers. With a
taut, humming song, long straight shafts were loosed and
barbed death struck the advancing reptiles.

And the first arrow caught Captain Raphad straight between the eyes. . . .

Yualla and Murg continued on across the plains, drawing

ever nearer to the range of mountains known as the Walls of Zar. The girl maintained a rapid, limber, space-eating stride, for she was impatient to join forces with Hurok and the other warriors, and reluctant to miss any of the excitement of this adventure which she had impulsively determined to share.

Murg, his bony wrists lashed together behind his back, a noose about his throat, must perforce trot along behind the cave-girl. This was because she bore one end of the tether about his neck in her small, capable fist. If he failed to keep up with her, he might well be strangled.

Or so Murg feared. Actually, the girl was too tender-hearted (at least as concerned enemies she viewed with contempt, like Murg) to have let the miserable little man strangle.

Fortunately for Yualla and Murg, few beasts more dangerous than the plump, timid, and edible little uld roamed the plains this close to the Walls of Zar, for the larger and more ferocious predators were held at bay for fear of the mighty thodars. Although they are not vegetarians and not carnivores, the brontosaurs are so large and heavy that they can break the backs of lesser reptiles or even of the mighty mastodons and woolly mammoths by simply stepping on them—which reminds me of the time a triceratops had the Professor and me treed, during our first day or so in Zanthodon, and got into a fight with a woolly mammoth, which promptly broke the back of the triceratops in the very manner I have just described.*

Of all the beasts of Zanthodon the Underground World, one of the most fearless, as it is one of the most ferocious, is the mighty vandar or sabertooth tiger. Twice the size of the Bengal tigers of the Upper World is this sleek, tawny, vicious brute, whose powerful jaws, armed with the formidable foot-long fangs which give the monster its name, make it a deadly adversary even for the great saurians who share the jungle world with it.

One particular vandar, fully grown and weighing more than a percheron, was roaming the grasslands hungrily this day. The jungles which bordered the northern plains to the south were empty of game, and hunger gnawed at the vitals

* The incident to which Eric Carstairs alludes may be found in Chapters 5 and 6 of *Journey to the Underground World*, the first volume of these adventures.

of the giant cat. For many wakes it had not made its kill and now, goaded almost to the point of madness by the pangs of starvation, it had ventured out onto the broad plains in search of game. Doubtless, its small but cunning brain was teeming with images of the plump, inoffensive, and succulent uld which it knew were to be found aplenty amid the grassy plains beyond the jungle's verge.

That these plains were ruled by the little olive-hued men who rode upon the feared and mighty thodars was well known to the sabertooth. This knowledge suggested caution to the predator; but hunger has a logic which can supercede even knowledge. And, were the vandar to have been capable of human reason, it might well have reasoned thus: better to die swiftly and cleanly beneath the tread of the thodar, than to die meanly by inches from starvation.

Mad with hunger though it was, the vandar crept furtively upon the plains into the region of low hills and ravines which bordered upon the mountains. Here the ponderous, slow-moving thodars could not move about, save in certain pathways. By avoiding those paths, which, of course, savored pungently of the spoor and droppings of the huge reptiles, the vandar hoped to avoid a confrontation.

Keeping well to the shadows, clambering lithely over the boulders and broken rocks, the great cat glided through the hills, seeking the borders of the open plain. It paused atop a rounded knoll to taste the humid breeze with twitching, sensitive nostrils. The oily smell of thodars was upon the wind, for they were abroad today, tracking the Sotharian tribes. But the mouth-watering odors of tender uld also rode upon the brisk winds, and the sabertooth slavered as it caught the scent.

Abandoning cover, the great cat sprang down and slunk into the thickly grown meadow grass. As it prowled, snuffling the ground for uld spoor, another odor even more inviting came to its nostrils.

The scent of human flesh. . . .

The sabertooth had made human kills before, and in one corner of its bestial brain it warily knew that two-legged prey most often went armed with sharp and heavy rocks fastened in some mysterious fashion to the end of short sticks, or with throwing-sticks which were long and sharply pointed and could somehow kill from a distance.

But this knowledge lurked in one corner of the vandar's brain only, and all the rest of that organ was possessed to the point of madness by *hunger*. And so overwhelming had that

"In the next instant, a tawny form leaped like a
furry thunderbolt."

hunger become by now that it drowned out all caution in the
mind of the famished supertiger.

It tested the breeze, and found that it did not have to track
this new game, for the game was advancing upon it with
swift and eager strides.

The striped cat easily concealed itself in the cover of the
long grasses, and crouched, belly to the earth, tail-tip
twitching, ready to launch upon its terrible and irresistible
charge.

The earth trembled slightly beneath its body, beating like a
drum from the impact of striding human feet. The vibration
was so slight that only a canny predator might have caught
and interpreted it, but the vandar was full-grown, a veteran
fighter, an experienced hunter, and could read that faint, far
drumming with ease.

It crouched, tension gathering in the coiled and steely
muscles of its lean hindquarters.

The game was only instants away now, and the vandar was
crouched in the concealing grasses directly in its path. . . .

Yualla came across the grasses toward the first of the hills
with a light, rapid pace, poor Murg wheezing and puffing as
he trotted along in her wake.

The girl did not even have time to scream as the thick
grasses parted to reveal a hideous face distorted in a snarl of
fury.

In the next instant a tawny form hurtled upon her like a
furry thunderbolt.

Chapter 20

THEY REACH ZAR

Hurok stood, heavy arms folded upon his hairy breast, and stared down thoughtfully into the valley of the inland sea. There before him stretched the immensity of Zar, the Scarlet City of the Minoans. And what a spectacle it was!

Never in all of his days had the mighty Neanderthal of Kor seen a city. Never had he even imagined one. All he knew was Kor, land of the Apemen, with its caves burrowed into the cliffs, and the jungle country of Thandar and the other Cro-Magnon nations, and the cavern-city of the Gorpaks and the ghastly Sluaggh.

He was impressed in spite of himself, was Hurok the Apeman. The massive structures were obviously man-made, looming two or three stories into the air, spired with squat, four-sided towers and slim obelisks. Toward the central parts of the Scarlet City loomed the palace citadel atop its high place, perhaps the most stupendous mass of masonry ever erected within Zanthodon the Underground World.

Dim, small eyes peering and blinking beneath the heavy shelf of his bony brows, the apelike Neanderthal slowly looked over the city . . . the streets and boulevards and avenues and narrow, dark alleys between the looming piles of masonry . . . the squares and forums and bazaars, like open glades or clearings amid the forest of buildings . . . the palaces and temples, mansions and warehouses, fortresses and barracks . . . and, beyond, the vast, walled, seat-ringed oval that was the mighty arena. . . .

Fantastic and bizarre were the decorations which ornamented the city: friezes and mosaics, tapestries and banners, statues and idols and stone monsters, carven masks and leering dragons, the glitter of glazed tile, the rich mingling of brazen colors flaunting their brilliance back in the face of daylight . . . the throng which surged to and fro in the streets, ragged

125

beggars whining for alms, fat-bellied merchants squatting on bits of carpet under striped awnings, guardsmen alert and vigilant atop the towers, daylight flashing from gilt helm and spear-blade and trident . . . veiled women glimpsed in swinging palanquins borne on the brawny shoulders of blond slaves . . . fountains playing, rooftop gardens. . . .

And upon the breast of the inland sea itself, the watery moat which guarded Zar from its enemies no less staunchly than did the sheltering wall of mountains, ships bobbed at anchor: pleasure craft glided to and fro, laden with blossoms and girls . . . stern, brass-beaked war triremes lashed to the end of stone piers . . . merchant ships, as fat-bellied as their owners, plied the bright waters, hulls crammed with casks of red wine and wild honey, chests of gems and worked brass and carven ivory hewn from the curlicue tusks of mammoths, bales of cotton, rolled-up carpets, tin pots, ripe fruits, bales of golden grain—

Hurok blinked, and rubbed his eyes, dazed and bedazzled at the complexity, the colors, the sheer, inconceivable newness of so much in the busy, bustling, gaudy, magnificent scene which stretched far beneath where he stood on the farther slopes of the mountain range.

Behind and about him, his warriors crouched and stared, with much the same awe and amazement that filled his mighty breast. For the Cro-Magnon warriors of Sothar and distant Thandar dwelt, for the better part, in bamboo huts or long, rambling, low-roofed structures which resembled log cabins. Only the High House of the Omad was taller, a two-storied building which had heretofore seemed to their simple imaginations the most impressive structures of which human hands were capable.

And now they looked for the first time upon one of the last cities in the world wherein the grandeur and might of the ancient world could still be seen. Only, perhaps, in the ruins of Pompeii or Knossos could the magnificence of the mighty past be glimpsed, and only in part, the gaps in those ruins pieced together by the magic of imagination. But here was one of the oldest cities of the world, surviving in all its fantastic richness and color!

"O Hurok," muttered Varak from his side in dazed, low tones, "how can we ever hope to find Eric Carstairs and the old man in all of . . . *that*?"

The Neanderthal shook his heavy, low-browed head ponderously, choosing silence over speech. He could not have said what he had expected to find—a valley whose cliff walls were pocked by caves, perhaps, or a palisade-walled cluster of wood huts, such as he had seen on slave-raiding expeditions into Thandar and Gorad and Numitor and other Cro-Magnon lands.

But he could never have imagined anything like *this*.

"What shall we do, my chieftain?" muttered Erdon helplessly, from where he stood beside his brother-in-arms, Ragor. "We are six warriors against many, many times that number. How can we do battle against so many, or find our way to the side of Eric Carstairs amid that—that wilderness of colored stone?"

The Apeman of Kor spoke up then, but with his customary brevity.

"We can but try," he said dully. "For at least to try is what Black Hair would expect of us. Not—miracles. . . ."

"There are sentinels atop the taller structures," observed Warza, pointing. "They will have been chosen for their posts by alertness and vigilance, to say nothing of possessing the sharp eyes of hunting hawks. And they will see us as we descend the slope."

"Then we shall conceal ourselves as best we may," grunted Hurok, "and descend the slope with care, taking advantage of such cover as we may find."

"And then?" demanded Parthon the Sotharian. "How can we enter the city? True, it is not guarded by a palisade, but see how the buildings crowd together, with but narrow ways between. Surely, these are guarded!"

"And how shall we be able to swim the moat, for in truth it is more than a lake, this place, almost a sea!" cried Varak impatiently. "The stone bridges are guarded—see? And there? Can mere men swim so far unseen?"

"They will slay us with arrows before we have swum even half the distance to the island," muttered Ragor gloomily.

Hurok shrugged his burly, anthropoid shoulders irritably. Idle talk always depressed and annoyed him, for he preferred the more direct and simple course—taking bold action, rather than endlessly talking about which action to take.

"We shall swim beneath the wider of the stone bridges," he rumbled. "Men cannot see through the solid floor beneath their feet. The bridge is supported upon pilings sunk into the floor of the sea, and there are struts of heavy logs built between the pilings to brace and strengthen them: upon these shall we rest when we become weary from so long a swim. . . ."

"But—I have heard that Hurok of Kor knows not how to swim!" cried Erdon, remembering my account of how I had once saved the Korian from death by drowning when a great yith (or plesiosaurus) overturned a dugout canoe.*

"That is true," admitted Hurok somberly.

"How then will Hurok swim the waters of the sea?" inquired the other. The Apeman of Kor shook his head dumbly.

"Perhaps Hurok will learn by doing," he said.

The others looked at one another, questioningly. They had learned to swim as boys in jungle rivers and in the many lakes which dotted the countryside. And they remembered that the skill was not all that swiftly or easily acquired. . . .

"We shall have to have Hurok sit upon a log large and light enough not to sink beneath his weight, and steer him along by swimming beside the log, guiding it with one hand," suggested Varak to his companions.

"Hurok will not do it," said that worthy in firm tones. The very notion of squatting gingerly atop a fallen tree, being towed along by his warriors, while they twisted through the water, lithe and supple as so many eels, would tend to make anyone feel ridiculous. And Hurok had a very well-developed sense of personal dignity.

"Hurok must do it, or something very like it, if he is to cross the moat with us," Parthon pointed out.

Grumbling and growling to himself, the Neanderthal subsided into a lame silence.

They waited for his acknowledgment that they were right. But none came, as the Apeman maintained a stubborn, truculent mien.

"What does Hurok say?" Warza asked at last.

"Hurok says: let us climb down the slope, and leave crossing the moat to the moment when we are face-to-face with that problem," growled Hurok shortly. "Perhaps, with any luck, Hurok will trip and fall down the mountainside, and break his neck!"

* A description of this scene will be found in Chapter 12 of *Journey to the Underground World.* I am unable to explain why the Neanderthals, who dwell on the island of Ganadol, which, like all islands, is completely surrounded by water, are not able to swim. Perhaps it is due to their great weight, or extreme clumsiness, or a simple, primitive fear of drowning. Perhaps a combination of all three.

Grinning, but avoiding his angry eye, they began with great care and caution to descend the mountainside, taking every advantage of cover and concealment which presented itself. From time to time a diversion occurred: two galleys collided in the midst of the lake-like sea, starting a loud argument between the two merchant skippers, which attracted the amused attention of everyone within earshot and eye-reach.

The warriors took advantage of this noisy incident to sprint a good way down the slope, flinging themselves into the bushes as the argument began to subside.

A bit later, three thakdols soared over the inland sea at an unusually low height, providing another diversion. The warriors got down into the lake up to their necks and waded along the offshore area until the width of the bridge concealed them beneath it.

"That was close," muttered Parthon grimly.

"Yes, but I would enjoy thanking those thakdols personally," quipped the irrepressible Varak.

"There's a good log, O Hurok," said Ragor, pointing to the trunk of a fallen tree which had become lodged among the pilings which supported the end of the bridge. Hurok looked gloomy.

But not so gloomy as he looked when, a bit later, he sat hunched atop that very log, clinging for dear life to the stubs of broken-off branches, as six grinning warriors steered him across the lake with many a humorous remark at his expense.

Part Five

---•—◆—•---

THE
THUNDER-
WEAPON

Chapter 21

I BREAK OUT OF JAIL

Following the unsatisfactory conclusion of my private interview with the Empress, I found myself being escorted to a new suite in another part of the palace. I was left alone there, kept under strict guard, although every courtesy was shown me and my prison cell was luxurious.

It bothered me that I could not see the Professor. The old geezer and I had been through some interesting times together, and had shared some remarkable experiences and adventures. No one would answer me when I asked why I could not see my friend, and I was not again summoned into the presence of Zarys.

I was more than a little thankful for *that*.

And I was more than a little anxious about the meaning of all of this. When I discovered that Zarys had my automatic, many things fell into place like the pieces of a puzzle. Obviously, that wily rascal, Xask, had been busily at work behind the scenes, and the attempted seduction—or whatever it was—had been a try at winning my cooperation in the manufacture of the thunder-weapon.

Zarys was no fool: she must have known from my words and my manner that there was no real hope of coercing or coaxing me into revealing the secret. But why was I being kept apart from Professor Potter?

I fretted the long days of my captivity away. Perhaps "captivity" is the wrong word to use for a sumptuous and airy apartment crammed with gorgeous tapestries and wall-paintings, adorned with perfumed lamps and silken cushions, where I dined splendidly on the rarest and most succulent foods and wines.

If this was what being in jail was like in Zar, thought I to myself, I'll take it to being in jail anywhere else in the world.

Since my repeated requests for an interview with Zarys or

133

Hassib the Grand Panjandrum fell on deaf ears, after a week
or so of this sort of kid-gloves treatment, I resolved to take
things into my own hands. One "night" I climbed out on the
narrow ornamental balcony of the window in my room and secured one end of a long line to the railing of carven stone.

I had manufactured this line by knotting together strips of
strong cloth torn from my surplus bedding. Not having been
able to give my handiwork a genuine test, I prayed to whatever gods watch over crazy adventurers like myself, and
clambered down the line. About thirteen feet beneath my
windowsill a stone ledge ran along the outer wall, parallel to
the parks and grounds below. It was there purely for decoration, but I thought it looked strong enough to bear my
weight. . . .

It was.

But it was only about fourteen inches wide. I crept along
it, inching my way with my shoulders pressed flat against the
outer wall and feeling my way along with bare toes.

I tried not to look down. I've always had an average head
for heights, which is to say I would have made a mediocre-
to-crummy mountain climber. But vertigo is an affliction to
which the human animal is universally subject, and I tried to
keep cool. Which makes me laugh, thinking back on that
dreadful trip, for all the while I was sweating like a bull.

In the perpetual noontime of Zanthodon anyone who cared
to glance up could have discovered me inching my way
along the wall, and probably would have roused the gen-
darmes to pry me off it. Gardeners toiled beneath my feet,
trimming hedges, spading moist earth, and doing the other
grubby little things that keep gardeners busy. But not one of
them turned to look at me.

After what seemed like about half an eternity, I found the
ledge had brought me within arm's length of another balcony
and another window. Risking much, I peered in and discovered the room to be empty. Not only that, but it seemed un-
tenanted as well, for the couch was stripped of bedding and
the carpets were rolled up and stacked against the farther
wall. I climbed in through the window and tested the door. It
was locked from the outside—naturally, I suppose.

I set my shoulder against it and heaved. Nothing happened.
Another heave, and a bit more muscle behind it this time.
Something within the lock mechanism went KRAK!, and I
opened the door ever so slightly and peered both ways. The
corridor was empty.

Moving on quick, light feet, I went down the hall, choosing a direction at random. I was by now completely disoriented and had no idea where I was. I also began to curse myself for taking such a chance, as the first person to come along would spot me as an escaping prisoner and would sound the alarm.

Well, what the hay! So long as your captors want something out of you, they're not very likely to feed you to the cobras for a minor transgression. And—aren't prisoners supposed to try to escape, anyway?

The slap of leathern sandals up ahead, around the curve of the hallway, alerted me. I just barely had time to conceal myself behind a heavy tapestry before a squadron of palace guards went clanking by. I felt mighty grateful that the Minoans seemed unusually fond of wall-hangings, because over the next two hours of my prowl through the palace, I was able to avoid discovery and capture by taking similar refuge about six times.

I had timed my expedition to a fine degree: it would be four hours before the next meal was brought to me, which gave me a comfortable margin of time to cover as much ground as possible before beating (hopefully) a retreat and regaining my rooms before the maids came in.

What I hadn't figured on was that the palace was as large and as complicated as it turned out to be. I had thought that, with a little diligent prowling, I would soon encounter familiar territory and find the apartments in which the Professor and I had first been situated, and in which the old fellow was presumably still staying.

After two solid hours of searching, I had to abandon my plan. I simply didn't find anything that looked familiar.

I was about to turn back, retrace my steps, get back up my line and give it up for this time, anyway, when the unexpected happened. I say "unexpected," but actually I should have expected it.

I turned a corner and walked smack into a girl!

With a frightened squeak, she dropped to her knees and bumped her forehead against the floor. Looking down, I saw that she wore the slave collar of a palace servant.

Then she looked up timidly, obviously fearing that she had collided with a snooty member of the local aristocracy, and I had another shock. I knew her!

It was Ialys, the Empress's handmaiden. . . .

I must have looked about as flustered and tongue-tied as I felt, for her expression of surprise swiftly gave way to one of sly amusement. She rose to her feet and saluted me deferentially.

"Is the Lord Eric taking a bit of a stroll?" she inquired demurely.

I shrugged, forcing a laugh which rang false even to my ears.

"You've got me!" I said. "Actually, I wasn't really trying to escape; I was just trying to find my friend—you know, the old man with the little white beard?"

She nodded, humor dancing impishly in her eyes.

"Has the Goddess given her noble guest the freedom of the Great House?" she asked. "If so, Ialys has heard nothing of this. . . ."

"I'm afraid not," I confessed with a grin. "I sort of took it on myself to go for a walk. And I'd be eternally grateful, Ialys, if you wouldn't give me away. I'm honestly not trying to escape."

Her expression sobered. She examined me thoughtfully.

"When the Goddess commanded that you use the thunder-weapon upon her handmaiden, why did you dare to refuse?" she asked.

I cleared my throat awkwardly.

"Like I said at the time," I muttered, "I'm not used to killing nice people in cold blood."

"But Ialys is not a 'person,' she is a slave." She said this with a questioning lilt in her voice, and her eyes were puzzled. In her world, I gathered, one does not risk disobedience to goddesses—and certainly not over one so lowly and unimportant as a mere slave.

"In my country, there are no slaves," I commented. "Oh, sure, we had them once, to our eternal regret and guiltiness. But the wisest and most humanitarian of our statesmen and philosophers taught us that no person has the right to own another person. And in my country it is against the law to own a slave. . . ."

Her face expressed her wonderment, and the emotion in her beautiful eyes was all but unreadable. Tears welled up but were quickly suppressed.

"Ialys could wish that she had been born in your country," she said wistfully.

I nodded, saying nothing, for there was nothing I could think to say. She studied me for a long, long moment, her face inscrutable. Then, before I could stop her, she took my hand and pressed her lips against the back of it.

"What was *that* for?" I demanded, flushing.

A sad smile touched her warm lips.

"For having the courage and the manliness to spare the life of a worthless slave," she said softly.

"No human life is worthless," I said stoutly.

"Is that another wise teaching from the philosophers of your country?"

"I believe it is."

"They breed wise men in that far land," she observed. "And brave and gallant men, too."

"They do that."

Her eyes were inscrutable. But from the way she squared her shoulders and took in a deep breath, I gathered that Ialys had reached a decision. She took my hand again, but not to kiss it this time.

"Come," she said simply. "I will take you to your friend. But Ialys fears that the Lord Eric will not at all like what he is about to see. . . ."

A cold stab of fear went through my vitals at that. But I set my jaw grimly and let her lead me to the Professor.

Chapter 22

JORN TO THE RESCUE

When Jorn emerged from the ravines which twisted between the low hills, his gaze fell upon a spectacle which astonished him.

There, trotting at a rapid pace directly toward him were the young Sotharian girl, Yualla, and the runaway, Murg. Jorn did not at once notice that Murg's hands were bound behind his back and that the cave-girl was leading him along like a dog on a leash.

This he did not have time to notice because of what else met his gaze.

Directly in front of him, with its back toward him, a gigantic sabertooth tiger crouched in the concealment of the long grasses.

The girl did not see Jorn, who stood in the shadows. Neither did she apparently see the giant vandar, crouched belly to earth concealed in the long meadow grasses. But Jorn took the entire situation in with a single sweeping glance.

The young hunter knew the vandar was about to pounce upon the Sotharian girl. He knew this from the way the muscles in its hindquarters were bunched with tension, and from the restless twitching of its tail-tip.

Jorn had hunted vandars in his native land, and knew well their habits. Within a split second, the beast would leap upon the girl and dash out her brains with a single swipe of its mighty paws. They were as heavy as sledgehammers, those velvet paws.

And Jorn was unarmed. . . .

Nevertheless, he did not for the slightest fraction of a second hesitate in what he next did. Chivalry is innate in the human breast, it seems, as the Cro-Magnons—who happen to be just about the finest people I have ever encountered—were very much human.

138

With a wild, crazy yell, the boy leaped full upon the back of the giant cat just as it began its lunge for the girl.

He landed between its shoulders; locking his legs about the barrel of the cat, he clung with both arms tight around the beast's neck and buried his face in the coarse, dry fur at the base of its throat.

Startled by the unexpected weight upon its back, the vandar's leap miscarried. It sprang to one side, missing the amazed Yualla, landing lightly on the turf. The weight of its unwanted burden, and the maddening man-smell, drove the sabertooth into a frenzy. It rolled over on its back, seeking to crush its rider beneath its weight. Fortunately, the grass was long and thick here, and very springy; all this maneuver accomplished was to drive the air out of Jorn's lungs.

Regaining its feet, the great cat sprang into the air, landing heavily. Obviously, it hoped to jar the grip of its rider loose. This, too, failed.

Next it attempted to reach back with snapping jaws and rip the offending weight from its shoulders. Those hideous ivory fangs clashed within mere inches of the boy's face. Its stinking breath blew foul in his nostrils, and gobbets of foam from its dripping jaws splattered his neck and shoulders.

Through it all, Jorn clung grimly to the back of the beast as one clings for dear life to a log in a maelstrom.

The paralyzing shock which froze Yualla proved only momentary. An instant later, the girl dropped Murg's tether and whipped up her bow, a weapon with which she was extremely expert. Time and time again she sought to loose a shaft into the belly or side of the rampaging sabertooth, but each time she faltered, fearing to transfix her rescuer with the shaft.

Moments later she saw her opportunity, and trained reflexes took command with the swift surety of instinct. She sank an arrow to the feather in the fleshy underpart of the beast's throat, just below the jaw.

Coughing blood, the brute shook its head, dazedly; then, mad with pain and fury, it gave voice to a thunderous yowl and hurtled toward her.

Yualla stood her ground just long enough to loose a second shaft, then threw herself to one side. The great cat stormed by, missing her so narrowly that its harsh fur brushed her bare legs. It wheeled to come at her again, a striped juggernaut of tawny-furred death—then reeled, lurched, and fell heavily on its side.

It lay there, panting raggedly, dribbling hot gore from between open, distended jaws.

Then it heaved one great sigh, and its eyes glazed, and it lay still.

The second arrow had caught the sabertooth directly in the left eye and had driven its cruel barb deep into the brain.

Crying and shaking like a leaf, Yualla half-dragged, half-shoved the dead weight of the vandar off Jorn's leg and helped him to his feet. He was shaken and stunned, bruised and battered, but otherwise unhurt.

When both boy and girl had recovered themselves and had regained a modicum of calm, they regarded each other somewhat warily.

"Jorn of Thandar, the Hunter, is grateful to the gomad Yualla for her assistance in slaying the beast," the boy said solemnly.

"Yualla of Sothar is grateful to Jorn the Hunter for risking his life to save her own," the girl replied with equal solemnity.

These ceremonial exchanges of gratitude done with, her eyes flashed angrily.

"What does Jorn *mean*—'assisting' in slaying the beast?" she demanded scornfully, staring obviously at his hands. "Did Jorn the Hunter hope to slay the vandar with his bare teeth or with his naked hands?"

The boy began an angry retort, then subsided, blushing, with a shamefaced grin.

"The gomad Yualla is correct," he admitted. "I had no hope of slaying the vandar. At the time, it did not occur to me that I had lost my weapons. I . . . only did what needed to be done," he finished lamely.

Her eyes glowed. Her expression softened. Her cheeks went bright pink.

"It was very, *very* brave of you," she whispered.

"It was nothing, really," said Jorn around a huge lump which had suddenly come into his throat from wherever it is that lumps in the throat of adolescent boys come.

She smiled shyly.

He stared deeply into her beautiful eyes . . .

Quite some time later, they remembered about Murg. With a little searching, they found the scrawny one crouched on his bony hunkers in the grass, eyes squeezed tightly shut.

"Is it you, m-mistress . . . or the b-beast?" he squeaked fearfully, sensing their nearness.

The girl grinned impishly, and made a growling, catlike sound deep in her throat.

Murg paled to about as pale a hue as one covered with dirt can pale, and shivered miserably.

They helped him to his feet, dusted him off, and cut his bonds. Now that Jorn had joined the party, Yualla feared nothing from the miserable little man.

Then they set off toward the mountains to rejoin Hurok and the others, if possible.

As Jorn, Yualla, and Murg followed a winding path through the foothills and began to ascend the slopes of the mountains, they broke the monotony of their journey with conversation. In fact, they narrated to each other in turn the story of their recent adventures.

The young huntsman was astonished to hear of the manner in which the thakdol had carried off the Sotharian girl, and was even more astonished that she had survived the adventure with neither hurt nor harm.

For her part, Yualla was impressed that Jorn had managed to live through the landslide, to say nothing of the lengthy and dangerous dive into the little mountain lake. Her estimate of the courage and stamina of the Cro-Magnon boy— which was already high, since his incredible feat of attacking the giant sabertooth tiger—rose all the more. It verged, perhaps, on idolatry; and the gomad of Sothar was not easily impressed by the male sex, being adventurous and daring to a fault herself.

The boy and the girl got along famously, exchanging information and getting to know one another. As for poor, miserable Murg, however, he plodded along, sniffing and snuffling, groaning with weariness from time to time, and feeling very, very sorry for himself. The two ignored him as much as was possible, the girl with frosty and aloof scorn, the boy with utter detestation. Rape is a crime not unknown to the Cro-Magnon tribes, of course, but one severely frowned upon as unmanly and displaying the vilest traits of cowardice.

From Murg in turn, however, during a pause to rest their aching leg muscles, the young people elicited an account of his own experiences since being captured by One-Eye. I suspect, as did they, that the account was rather heavily censored, if not considerably rewritten. It was ever the way of

Murg to vainly attempt to conceal his faults and flaws and
weaknesses by lies, deceits, and a certain application of sooth-
ing cosmetics to the plain unvarnished truth.

He did not really fool them, however. Both Jorn and
Yualla were clever enough to see through the abridged and
retouched portions of his narrative, and his pitiable attempt
at embellishment they found wryly amusing.

"To hear Murg tell the tale," murmured Jorn to the jungle
girl at his side, "he fled from Hurok's encampment with nothing but the noblest of motives in mind." The girl chuckled.
For indeed Murg had striven to convince his captors that he
had crept away from the sleeping place in order not to burden the stronger, swifter warriors with his less hardy presence.

Which hardly explained his thefts of the sleeping-hides,
water bottles, extra buskins, and surplus weapons, of course.

As Jorn was unarmed, he pressed the stolen armament into
service. It made him feel naked to be unarmed, and even
though he resolved to return the stolen property to its owners
as soon as they had caught up to Hurok and the others, he
intended in the meantime to put the weapons to good use.

They continued on their journey.

They began to climb the mountains.

Chapter 23

THE MYSTERIOUS CIRCLET

When the Cro-Magnon arrow struck Captain Raphad between the eyes he uttered a shrill cry and fell from the back of his enormous steed.

Moments later, he got shakily to his feet, stunned and dizzy, but otherwise unharmed.

The arrow had struck the circlet of shining metal which he wore upon his brows, and had dislodged the narrow band. Outside of giving him a headache, the lucky shot had done no harm.

Rubbing his aching forehead, he peered about him. And discovered the most surprising events taking place. . . .

Kicking and pounding the sides of their mounts and tugging furiously upon the reins, his squadron of riders seemed unable to command their docile beasts. What had been, only a moment before, a disciplined line-of-charge had now mysteriously decayed. The thodars had broken ranks and were wandering to and fro, placidly browsing upon the thick, lush meadow grasses, indifferent or perhaps actually oblivious to the furious commands of their human riders. Some had wandered off into the plains, perhaps in search of water. The battle, if so brief a skirmish can be thus properly described, was over.

As for the warriors of Sothar, they had also broken formation and were striding among the beasts, unceremoniously pulling the Zarians out of the saddle and binding their arms behind their backs. More than a few of the Dragon-riders had attempted to defend themselves against the savages, but the Cro-Magnons were taller, brawnier, and stronger than their diminutive adversaries and swiftly disarmed them with ease.

Garth came striding up to where Raphad stood, swaying dizzily, peering about in extreme puzzlement. The giant chief disarmed the Zarian officer and bound him in the same manner as his men were being bound. Nor did Raphad, who was no fool, attempt to resist; as good a soldier as the Scarlet City possessed, he recognized defeat.

Not that it tasted any better this time around. . . .

Then Garth stooped to pick up the fallen circlet. He turned it this way and that in his heavy, powerful hands, studying it curiously. As an ornament it was attractive, but there seemed more to the device than mere beauty of workmanship. For Garth had keenly observed that the very instant the circlet had been struck from Captain Raphad's brows, the advancing half-circle of giant reptiles had evaded the control of their human masters.

Garth was no more and no less superstitious than other savages of his degree of civilization. He supposed when he thought about it, which was very seldom, that he believed in ghosts and curses and (what was more to the point in this case), in magic.

It seemed to him that, somehow, possession of the circlet had enabled the leader of the enemy troop to control the enormous thodars. And he decided that it must therefore be a magical talisman. Having decided this, Garth carefully tucked away the circlet within the hide garments he wore.

Noticing this, Raphad bit his nether lip sourly.

Obviously, the Cro-Magnon leader thought the magic circlet might come in handy on some other occasion. And this was bad news indeed for Raphad and his people. . . .

The fact of the matter was, as Garth of Sothar imagined it to be, that possession of the circlet did indeed give the man who wore it a mysterious power to control the great reptiles.

When Raphad had, considerably earlier on, captured myself, Xask, and Professor Potter, the old scientist had sharply observed the uncanny circlet. And—as always!—he had evolved a theory concerning it.

The metal of the circlet was of a peculiar composition, ruddy yet gleaming. It seemed to be some sort of an alloy, perhaps the mixture of silver and copper. Both metals, the Professor knew, are excellent conductors of electrical impulses. And it had logically occurred to the scrawny savant that *thought itself* is nothing more than an electrical impulse, albeit one which is very feeble.

Centering between the brows of its wearer, the circlet bore a large cut piece of crystal. From these observations, the Professor theorized that the metal band somehow conducted the impulses of thought, which were *focused* by means of the crystal exactly as light is focused by a lens, and that in this manner the leader of the Dragon-riders maintained control of the beasts which he and his men rode through mental telepathy.

Had the Professor been present on this particular occasion, it would doubtless have delighted him to obtain practical verification of his tentative theory. For the very moment the circlet fell from the brows of the squadron leader, he and his men totally lost control of their reptilian mounts, which instantly reverted to their normal behavior.

I have neglected to mention another observation which had occurred to Professor Potter at the time. That mysterious alloy of reddish-silvery metal sounded very much like the unknown metal orichalc, the mystery metal of Lost Atlantis of which the Greek philosopher Plato spoke in his celebrated Atlantean dialogues, *Critias* and *Timaeus*.

The identity of the mysterious metal has never satisfactorily been determined by science. But, then, neither has the location of the fabled Lost Continent of Atlantis, itself.

But more recently, some scholars have tentatively established a connection between the legendary Atlantis and the very real island of Minoan Crete. And if the story of Atlantis sprang from the Greeks' half-remembered traditions of ancient Crete, and the uncanny orichalc of Atlantis was the same as the strange alloy of Raphad's circlet, then quite a few pages of material hitherto missing from the history books could be sketched in. . . .

Before the Underground World was very much older, Garth's warriors had secured and disarmed the Zarians and were ready for further instructions from their High Chief.

As for the thodars, the immense and placid beasts had all wandered off by this time, and were cropping the grasses here and there about the plains.

"What are your commands, my Omad, regarding the prisoners?" inquired one of Garth's chieftains. With a gesture he indicated the bound Zarians, who were looking extremely unhappy, as well they might.

Garth studied them, thoughtfully. The Cro-Magnon tribes were not accustomed to the slaughtering of helpless prisoners, but neither did their traditions demand that a war party encumber itself and retard its maneuverability by burdening itself with unwanted and useless guests. Unable any longer to

control their mounts, which in any case had now wandered
well out of reach, they offered no possible threat to the security of the Sotharian host.

And yet, to set the prisoners free might well give them an
opportunity to carry the warning of the Sotharian advance
back to Zar in time for the legions of the Scarlet City to
mount a vast force against them.

Garth had no particular reason for wishing to invade the
country of the Zarians, and, although he was unafraid of the
possibility of a battle, it was prudent to avoid one if this
could be done. All he was interested in was in finding his lost
daughter, Yualla, who had been carried off by the pterodactyl.

As was his way, the jungle monarch swiftly made up his
mind.

"Keep them guarded closely and see that not one Zarian
escapes to bring the word of our approach back to Zar, lest
they rouse a great force against us," he commanded. "We
shall at once resume the march to the mountains, in order to
search for the gomad Yualla. Pass these orders along. . . ."

The chieftains saluted and marched the prisoners off. Captain Raphad cast one sad glance behind him as he was forced
to accompany his warriors into captivity. If he could somehow purloin the circlet from the savage chief, it might be
possible even now—and at this distance—to regain control
over the mighty thodars. . . .

There seemed, however, no opportunity of doing this. But
Raphad decided to bide his time and keep his eyes and ears
open. In low tones he instructed his soldiers to obey the savages instantly and to avoid any trouble. The more the Cro-
Magnons thought him and his men cowed and demoralized
and helpless, the less attention they would give to guarding
them.

And that meant the more chance Raphad might have to escape and regain the circlet, although he knew in his heart of
hearts that he would have to murder Garth in order to get his
hands on it.

The host of Sothar marched across the plains and approached the mountains called the Wall of Zar.

If any further patrols of Dragon-riders had been sent forth
upon the plains, they saw no sign of them.

The keen gaze of Garth's scouts and huntsmen spotted the
nesting places of many thakdols upon the upper heights of

the mountains. So many of these could be discerned in the eternal midday light of Zanthodon that even the spirits of Garth were depressed. It might well take many weeks to search the nests of the pterodactyls, and the Sotharians were not accustomed to climbing mountains.

Garth discussed this problem with his chieftains when they gathered around the council fire before one sleep period.

"On this side, the slopes of the mountains are extremely steep, almost like vertical cliffs," one of the sub-chieftains pointed out. And perhaps I should explain at this point that the Sotharian host had come against the mountains a considerable distance from the place at which Hurok and his warriors had ascended the Walls of Zar. The mountainous terrain differed here from the part which Hurok had found, and was indeed much steeper.

"Does Kovor imply that the mountains might be easier to climb on the far side of the range?" asked Garth. The younger man shrugged and nodded.

"There is no way of knowing that, my Omad," he admitted. "But it is at least possible."

"So it is," rumbled the High Chief. "But to traverse the wall of mountains might consume many wakes and sleeps. And if the gomad Yualla yet lives, every moment might count."

At this point, one of the shrewdest of the Sotharian scouts spoke up.

"There is a pass through the mountains not far off, my Omad," he suggested. "It is low between the peaks, and from the shapes of the mountains on either side, it seems straight enough. Were we to take that route, we could perhaps be on the far side of the mountains before we next sleep."

Garth, too, had noticed the notch in the mountainous wall, but had thought little about it, as this problem had not presented itself before now.

Next "morning" the host marched toward the pass in question. For it was perfectly obvious that it would be an immensely difficult feat for the Sotharians to attempt to scale the mountains at this part of the range, and the suggestion of his counselors had persuaded the jungle monarch to cross the mountains first. Even though this meant invading the country of Zar. . . .

When Raphad discerned the direction in which the Cro-

Magnon tribe was headed, his shrewd eyes gleamed with satisfaction.

For the pass which was obviously the destination of the
savages was none other than the main pass into Zar, the one
of the stone monster heads.

And that pass was thoroughly guarded by unseen watch-
ers. . . .

Chapter 24

THE PROFESSOR'S INVENTION

Ialys had led me into an enormous stone-walled room filled with seething vapors, blazing furnaces, sulphurous stenches, and vile chemical reeks, where many artisans and workmen toiled. It was crowded, busy, and very noisy.

Hammers clanged on anvils, wielded by burly men stripped to the waist and black with soot. Sparks flew in showers from the strokes of their mauls and these, mingling with swirling clouds of black smoke, lent the cavernous room an aspect satanic, like a glimpse of the Inferno.

Amidst the noise and turmoil, my old friend Professor Percival P. Potter. Ph.D., hopped about shrilling orders, waving his arms excitedly, reprimanding or instructing his workmen in a feverish mixture of Zarian, Zanthodonian, and English.

He stopped short when he perceived me standing there at the entrance to this incredible basement factory.

"Eric, my boy! Holy Heisenberg, whatever are *you* doing here? I . . . I had thought you in chains, groaning under the cruel lash of these fiends. . . ."

I stared at him in utter bewilderment.

"What in the world—or under it!—are you talking about, Professor?" I demanded.

"Why—why—well," he spluttered, "Xask said—that is, I was given to understand. . . ."

"*Xask*, is it?" I said harshly, beginning to comprehend the astounding scene. "And you trusted a single word from that sly devil?"

"I—I—um," he muttered, subsiding feebly. And eyeing me more than a bit *guiltily*. . . .

Guiltily? Guilty about *what*?

I looked around me, eyes narrowing against the smoke. I

149

could smell the sulphur in the air, and there it was—heaps and mounds of raw yellow sulpher, being raked to and fro in long wooden trays. They were *purifying* the stuff.

Looking beyond, I saw open fireplaces where wood was obviously being reduced to charcoal.

And my heart sank within my breast. For I knew the ingredients of gunpowder as well as the Professor did. . . .

While I maintained a grim silence, the old boy showed me around. Since I had yet to utter a word of reproof, his natural buoyancy asserted itself. And he was obviously very proud of his work.

"I was presented with a host of problems, my boy, as you can doubtless well imagine . . . the Minoans are not yet into the iron age, although their technology is quite advanced; it is simply that this part of the mountain country seems lacking in iron ore. How, then, to fashion pistols or rifles? I resolved on case-hardened bronze, bound with brass wire to reduce the chances that the explosion of powder in the chamber might crack the barrels of the guns. . . ."

I nodded, saying nothing. The old boy's enthusiasm was so simple and pure, I did not wish to hurt his feelings by giving speech to the emotions I was feeling. Taking heart from my silence, he burbled on, proud as a peacock—

"The mechanism of a revolver is, I fear, a trifle too complex for the Zarian craftsmen, although, of course, in time . . . in time . . . at any rate, my dear boy, I simplified the design of my weapons to something like the old-fashioned blunderbuss, employing a lengthier barrel so as to build the velocity of the bullets and to improve, as much as is possible, the directness of their flight . . . it was a pretty problem, I assure you! But there was no way for these simpletons to rifle the inside of the barrels, if that is the proper word for it— *you* know what I mean, the inner spiral groovings which give a bullet the, ah, 'spin'. . . ."

He showed me the finished product. It was an ungainly cross between a Kentucky squirrel-hunter's rifle and a primitive blunderbuss. It looked ugly as hell, but I had little doubt that it would shoot well enough. The old flintlock rifles generally did. . . .

"The powder is crude enough, I know," he went burbling on, "and coarse, but as time goes on we shall undoubtedly be able to refine the mixture and reduce the size of the grains

. . . for bullets, now, I settled, after considerable thought, I can assure you, on simple slugs with cross-grooved noses—"

"Like dum-dum bullets?" I inquired heavily.

His watery blue eyes brightened cheerfully and his stiff little white spike of a goatee waggled as he nodded with enthusiasm.

"Precisely! I—ahem!—saw more than a few gangster movies in my younger years . . . the lead is easy enough to procure in these parts, fortunately. . . ."

I groaned inwardly. I had seen a few old gangster movies myself. And knew that a dum-dum bullet goes *in* easily enough, but when it comes out the other side, it leaves a hole large enough for a cat to walk through.

And we are talking about human bodies, not marksmen's targets.

"However did Xask talk you into this?" I asked, finally.

"Well, ah . . . the fellow presented me with some *very* cogent arguments, as I hope you realize," he faltered, evading my eyes. And then he went into a long and vague and rambling account of what Xask had said, which boiled down to very, very little.

Xask was an excellent con man. Like all con men, it's not the idea content of his sales spiel that counts, but the seeming honesty, vigor, and reasonableness of his voice and manner.

The Professor was honestly not able to recall the arguments and persuasions which the wily little Machiavelli had used to win him over. Except, of course, for the flat lie that I was in a damp, dripping cell, being worked upon daily by the torturers of Zar. . . .

Which suddenly made me understand why I had been escorted to an entirely new suite after my private interview with the Divine Zarys, rather than going back to bunk with the Professor. With me out of sight, Xask could tell the old man any lie he wanted to.

It was all very neat.

And very ugly.

Armed with these guns, the legions of Zar could overrun the entire length and breadth of the Underground World. No army had a chance of standing in their way. Picture the poor Cro-Magnons, with their bows and arrows, axes and spears, trying to stem an invading flood of Zarians armed with the Professor's flintlock rifles! Primitive and clumsy weapons though they were, they could cut down the boldest and most skillful of the warriors of Thandar or Sothar or any other tribe.

Including the Neanderthals of Kor—however many survived that massacre on the plains of the thandors—for all their ponderous might and savage ferocity.

Not even the Barbary Pirates could withstand the legions of Zar, no matter how strong their fortresses might be.

When you have gunpowder, you have rifles. It is a very short step from there to siege cannon. To catapult bombs. To grenades.

To world war. . . .

The Professor was chagrined when I finally pointed these things out to him. He looked crestfallen, lower lip wavering childishly, vague eyes filling with something suspiciously like tears. I tried to speak as reasonably and patiently as was possible under the circumstances, and I tried not to upbraid him, for I didn't want to hurt his feelings.

But my words must have been a crushing disappointment to the Prof. Like stepping on someone's bright new toy. And that's exactly what his flintlocks represented to him: not a weapon of war, of conquest, of sheer murder, but a bright, fascinating new toy.

The sheer, intellectual game of reinventing firearms, using ancient, traditional crafts and Bronze Age artisans had intrigued and captivated him. That the practical applications of his glittering new toys were nothing less than red murder, warfare, rapine, and plunder simply had not occurred to him. Or, if they had, it was but hazily, as a far off, distant possibility, outweighed by the excitement of the technical achievement.

I understood all of this, and tried not to speak harshly to the poor old fellow or to make him feel any worse than he did already. But plain facts had to be pointed out and, if necessary, driven home bluntly.

"Think of our brave and gallant friends facing a disciplined troop armed with these bright new guns of yours," I begged. "Think of Tharn and Varak and Garth and old Hurok . . . all of their bravery and gallantry and brute strength would be of no avail against what they call 'the thunder-weapon.' Of no avail at all."

"M-my boy," he quavered broken-heartedly. "I d-didn't think, I simply didn't think . . . why, Xask told me how the

Scarlet City is ringed about with savage foes, unable to defend itself, the warrior spirit fading out—"

"Come on, Doc, use your head!" I said roughly. "Those tame dinosaurs they ride are a dreadful weapon, better than Hannibal with his elephants, and a lot scarier."

"Y-yes, I believe you are right, I am indeed culpable. . . ."

"And to put such armaments within the grasp of sneaky rats like Xask—whom I wouldn't trust any farther than I could throw him, and I'd love to see just how far *that* would be!—or the Queen's pet general, our pal Cromus, remember him? As ambitious and as unscrupulous as they come—"

"You are quite right, my boy, and I deserve your harshest words. It was criminally negligent of me to have cooperated in the reinvention of firearms, intriguing experiment though it certainly was. But—what can I possibly do to stop it now? These Zarian engineers and bronzesmiths are cunning artificers, and swiftly grasped the principles I taught them . . . what could *I* do to change what has already been accomplished here?"

He had me stumped, and I had to admit it.

"I honestly don't know, Doc; but you've got to do *something*," I said. He looked troubled, but thoughtful: and when Professor Percival P. Potter, Ph.D. starts Thinking (with a captial 'T'), you can rest easier with the knowledge that you've got one of the best brains on (or under) the Earth working on your problem.

Ialys was tugging on my sleeve. I had almost forgotten she was there. She looked nervous and apprehensive.

"Lord Eric!" she cried. "You have stayed here too long—you must get back to your suite before the officers come—"

"What officers, girl?" I demanded.

"During every wake they come to inquire after the progress the old man, your friend, has achieved—*hurry!* I will escort you back to where we met."

I guess I had lost track of time, talking to the Doc. So I bade him a hasty adieu and let her hurry me to the door. But it was a little late for making a strategic withdrawal.

We ran straight into Cromus and his bully-boys.

Chapter 25

THE UNDERGROUND ROAD

Within the black mouth of an alley lithe figures lurked. Overtopping them by head and shoulders loomed a burly shape. Bewildered, they peered out upon a busy, noisy, bustling bazaar.

Hurok and his warriors had managed to reach the outskirts of the Scarlet City unobserved, by means of their trick of swimming beneath the stone bridge which connected the island of Zar with the shores of the inland sea. But from this point on, there seemed to be no way to penetrate more deeply into the Minoan city without risking the chance of discovery.

The alley was narrow and black as pitch, for tall buildings shut out the eternal daylight of the Underground. This darkness was unnatural to the Cro-Magnon men and it made them distinctly uneasy.

Neither did they enjoy the filth and stench of the narrow way, with its heaped and fetid garbage, its worn cobbles beslimed with ooze, its mouth choked with abandoned junk and fragments of debris. They were eager to be out of this dark, vile place—into the open air and daylight once again.

Hurok, however, cautioned against such rashness. What, after all, could a mere handful of men however bold and brave, hope to accomplish in a city filled with thousands of their enemies?

The gloom of the alley bothered the Neanderthal warrior little. Accustomed as he was to the dark caves of his rocky homeland of Kor on the island of Ganadol, his small and dim eyes rather enjoyed their brief respite from the all-pervading daylight of the surface of Zanthodon.

"How can we hope to do battle against so many?" he rumbled in his deep bass tones. "Only by stealth and with

154

great care could we dream of finding where Black Hair and the old man, his companion, are held. . . ."

"But where, O Hurok, in all this wilderness of stone caves would they imprison our chieftain?" asked Varak pointedly. "What use to linger here amid the blackness and the stench, when we have not the slightest idea of where Eric Carstairs lies imprisoned?"

There was good sense in Varak's words, as Hurok well knew. But the burly and hulking Apeman of Kor had a shrewd notion of where his black-haired friend could be found. From the cliffs he had studied the layout of the Scarlet City, and had noticed that toward the center of the metropolis a lofty palace or citadel reared its spires atop a rise of ground. Of course, Hurok had no acquaintance with cities, ancient or modern; he had no way of guessing that the highest part of ground within the circuit of most of the great cities of the ancient world had been chosen to house the most important structures. This was true of the Acropolis of Athens as it was true of the Capitoline of Rome and the Brysa of age-lost Carthage.

And it was also true of Zar, the Scarlet City of the Minoans. . . .

To Hurok's way of thinking, so important a prisoner as Black Hair would be held in the residence of the ruler of Zar. And that residence could only be the huge and imposing pile of masonry which rose on the hilly heights at the center of the city, with the great arena behind it. The problem was— how could he lead his warriors all that distance without their being seen and the alarm sounded?

And that was a problem indeed. . . .

Squatting on his heels, Hurok pondered his dilemma. And as he did so there came to his ears a gurgling as of running water. This sound seemed to come from a rust-eaten grill set into the cobbled surface of the narrow little alleyway. For what reason the barred opening had been built Hurok could not imagine; he had not, after all, ever heard of sewers and neither could he have known that ancient Knossos, capital of Crete, had been famous in antiquity for its running water and flush toilets.

And running water must run *somewhere*. . . .

Examining the grill, the Neanderthal warrior discovered that it could be lifted free of its iron frame. When he strove to accomplish this, he made the further discovery that ages of neglect had effectively welded the grill to its frame with layers of encrusted rust.

While his baffled men looked on in total lack of comprehension, Hurok bent all of his mighty strength to the task of wrenching free the grill of the sewer. Great thews swelled to rock hardness along his sloping and apelike shoulders; ropes and cables of muscle sprang into sharp relief along his broad back and deep, furred chest.

With a sharp *crack!* the layers of rust shattered and the grill came loose in his hands. Peering down into the opening he had made, the Apeman of Kor blinked as his eyes adjusted to the virtually impenetrable gloom of the sewer. Soon he discovered the opening to be a long, narrow tunnel one end of which obviously emptied into the inland sea, as it went in that direction.

Peering the other way, he glimpsed the continuation of the underground passage, as it rose ever so slightly, extending in the same direction as they wished to travel, toward the center of the great city.

The roof and walls of the tunnel were of dressed and fitted stone, and seemed secure enough as no fallen or crumbling blocks could be seen. Down the middle of the floor trickled a slimy stream of black water which reeked of human offal. If one could endure the darkness (he thought slowly to himself) and ignore the horrendous stench—and if the sewer tunnel truly extended as far as the palace citadel on the height, one could with luck and fortitude traverse the city unseen, by the remarkably simple expedient of traveling *beneath* it.

Slow-witted and unimaginative primitive Neanderthal though he certainly was, Hurok of Kor possessed a native shrewdness that sometimes serves one better in adversity than a dozen college degrees.

"What is it that Hurok has found?" inquired Parthon as his leader slowly straightened and turned to confront the little band.

A rare grin slowly stretched the thick lips of the Apeman. Humor and relief gleamed in his little sunken eyes.

"The pathway to the place where our chieftain lies in prison," he grunted.

The Cro-Magnon warriors blinked and stared at each other, then bent to regard the black opening in the alley's floor and the even blacker tunnel thus revealed.

They were troubled and dismayed; if the darkness of the narrow-walled alley had discomforted them, how could they endure the stench and the unbroken gloom of the underground road Hurok had found?

In low tones, rather ashamed of their complaining, they put this question to the great Neanderthal who had become their leader. He grinned again, and gave voice to a throaty chuckle.

"Are the warriors of Thandar and of Sothar children that they fear the darkness of a cave?" he inquired sarcastically. "If this is so, then let them employ the flints they carry to ignite a torch by whose illumination the darkness may be driven hence and they may see their way!"

"Flints we have, as Hurok knows," grumbled Warza sourly. "But torches we have not, as Hurok also knows. . . ."

The Apeman of Kor gestured with one mighty arm at the mounds of rotting garbage which blocked the mouth of the dark alley.

"There before Warza lie broken boxes and discarded rags," he said significantly. "Surely, one so clever as Warza can fashion therefrom a torch or two?"

Flushing a little at the implied rebuke, Warza bent to the task. Wrenching apart the slats of a broken crate, he wound one end with filthy rags. Flint struck fiery sparks when dashed against flint; with a little encouragement, the makeshift torch was set burning.

It burned smokily, true, sending a coil of sooty black smoke into the air. And the light it cast was fitful and even feeble. Still and all, it *was* light and would certainly serve to alleviate somewhat the gloom of the sewer tunnel.

One by one the warriors lowered themselves gingerly into the black mouth of the opening, finding themselves up to their ankles in dirty water and not quite able to stand erect. The torches Warza had fashioned shed a dim, wavering orange glow which disclosed to their eyes the gradually ascending tunnel that extended in the direction of the central parts of the Scarlet City.

Holding their breath against the fetid stench, they began to inch along. The stone trough which ran down the middle of the sewer tunnel was slimed with layers of ancient grease and mold and nameless ooze. It was uncomfortable not being able to stand erect, and the air was of vile quality.

Nevertheless, they went up the tunnel and began their unpleasant trip to the citadel of the Witch Queen of Zar, the Scarlet City.

"They began their unpleasant trip to the citadel
of the Witch Queen of Zar."

What they should find when they reached the end of the underground road none of them knew or could even guess. Perhaps, another grilled opening such as the one whereby they had entered into the sewer. Or perhaps a sheer pipe leading upwards into the structure of the palace, a vertical ascent which not even the nimblest or most agile of their number could hope to climb.

But, at every step of their quest to rescue Eric Carstairs and Professor Potter, they had faced up to and overcome obstacles which had, at the time, seemed unconquerable. By courage and strength, patience and ingenuity, they had come this far in their search for their captive chieftain.

And this was merely one more obstacle to be met and overcome. . . .

These thoughts passed slowly through the mind of Hurok of Kor as the mighty Apeman plodded through the underground tunnel. Like the true leader he was, like the actual leader he had become, the burly Neanderthal tried to foresee the hazards that might lie ahead, the dangers they might soon face, and the problems which the future might soon reveal, so as to plan a means of surmounting them.

Of course, not a man of them—not even Hurok—could possibly have guessed what they would face when they reached the end of the underground road. . . .

Part Six

---◆---◆---◆---

GODS
OF ZAR

Chapter 26

MY BLUFF FAILS

Cromus regarded me with blank astonishment. Obviously, the little commander had thought me safely mewed up in my silken, sumptuous cell. To find me here, in the secret factory where the Professor was busily reinventing firearms was about the last thing the pompous, strutting little bantam could have expected.

There was no hope of fighting my way through half-a-dozen armed men, so I resolved to try to bluff my way out of this predicament. Permitting no trace of my shock or consternation to show, I folded my arms across my breast and regarded the gaudy little officer with a casual smile.

"What do you here, prisoner?" demanded Cromus in harsh tones. I shrugged and turned upon him a serene and guileless gaze.

"The chosen lover of the Divine Zarys," I said blandly, "is free to come and go as he wishes in the palace of his beloved."

The features of Cromus darkened, flushing with anger and jealousy. His thin lips parted, then closed to stifle an angry retort. As he eyed me truculently and suspiciously, chewing his lower lip in obvious indecision, I realized my advantage.

Cromus knew very well that I had been granted private audience with the woman he desired. Palace scuttlebutt probably had it that I had been offered the love of Zarys. The frustrated and madly jealous heart of Cromus quite likely pictured the scenes which his tormented imagination painted—scenes of myself in the cool arms of Zarys, of myself pressing fiery kisses upon the moist and panting mouth of Zarys—scenes certainly calculated to do nothing to assuage or lessen his hatred of the man who had knocked him down before all of the assembled nobles.

Palace scandal doubtless also reported that I had scorned

the love of Zarys, and had been locked up for weeks in order
to meditate upon my refusal of her favors, and, perhaps, re-
pent.

However, to refuse the arms and lips of the Goddess was
something so incredible and unprecedented as to seem utterly
impossible to a rejected suitor such as Cromus. And now my
cool words confirming his darkest fancies, so that his acceptance of the rumor was deeply shaken.

"And now if the commander would kindly step aside, I
shall be on my way," I suggested. It couldn't do any harm to
try bluffing my way out of this, for I was already in enough
hot water to scald the toughest hide.

He eyed me dubiously, trying to make up his mind what to
do. Of course, it would hardly be wise for him to offer vio-
lence to the chosen lover of Zarys . . . on the other hand,
supposing that I lied, it would hardly be wise to let me go
scot-free.

It was a pretty problem!

Cromus solved it in such a way as to earn my admiration,
although I disliked the strutting popinjay almost as much as
he disliked me.

"Come, then," he grunted. "I and my soldiers will escort
the Lord Eric to the apartments of the Divine Empress as a,
ah, guard of honor. Surely, the Goddess will appreciate the
esteem and honor we will thus bestow upon her
chosen. . . ."

Then he shot me a sly and cunning glance.

"And surely the Lord Eric will not offend those who would
do honor unto him by refusing to accept that honor!"

Well, he had me there, all right! There was nothing that I
could think to do but nod with cool politeness and let the
guardsmen lead me through the corridors beyond the Professor's laboratory.

Ialys, looking pale and frightened, had perforce to accompany us. Two soldiers closed in on either side of the handmaiden so that she must walk between them.

My mind racing furiously as I strove to figure out some
way of getting out of this spot, I barely noticed the suites and
halls and stairways by which we traversed the bewildering
maze that was the palace citadel.

I didn't notice much of anything, in fact, until with a sudden shock I found myself standing before the veiled aperture
which led to the private apartments of the Empress.

Here we halted while Cromus strutted forward to exchange

a few words with the guard captain stationed before the door. These words were breathed in tones too low for my ears to catch their meaning. Saluting, the captain entered the suite and within a moment or two he returned.

"The Divine One will see you now," he said to Cromus. "*All* of you."

Within the boudoir of the Goddess, another shock awaited me. It certainly was turning out to be a day full of surprises. . . .

For the Empress, it seemed, was in her bath.

It was a sunken tub, tiled with pale jade and rich lapis lazuli, wherein she reclined in sudsy, perfumed water, reposing languidly while handmaidens as naked as was she gently laved her slender limbs.

She regarded us lazily, with a little smile. How beautiful she was I give my reader leave to imagine for himself. Her slim, bare limbs gleamed lustrously through the soapy water; foamy bubbles clung to her perfect, pointed breasts like pearls.

I hastily averted my eyes while Cromus, coming stiffly to attention, began making his report.

"Goddess, I found the Lord Eric in the workshop where the wise one toils at the fashioning of the thunder-weapon," he said. "Understanding that he had been made a prisoner by the command of Your Divinity, I inquired into his presence and learned from his lips that, as the chosen companion of the Divine Zarys, he might come and go as freely as he wished. Not daring to contradict one who might, indeed, be speaking the truth and be thus intimate with the Divine Presence, and therefore sacrosanct, I merely escorted the Lord hither to make this report."

He darted a snaky glance at Ialys who stood, white-faced and trembling, between two strong guards.

"And his accomplice, as well," he added.

The Empress studied me and the hapless girl for a long moment, the brilliance of her gaze veiled by silken lashes. Her expression was inscrutable.

"So, Eric Carstairs," she drawled at last in a lazy, purring voice, "you claim to be my lover? You boast to others of that relationship which was offered unto you, and which you so rashly declined? And, to make matters even worse, you have subverted—if not even seduced—my faithful handmaiden?"

I tried a bit of bluff again. Shrugging and grinning with a

touch of bravado, I said: "Well, I went for a little walk, I must admit! Gets awfully tiresome, locked up with nothing to do. As for Ialys, she had nothing to do with it. I just sort of ran into her along the way—"

Those magnificent eyes flashed dangerously.

"Do not dream that you can make a fool of the Divine Zarys with your flimsy lies!" she snapped. "Guiltiness is written upon the girl's face for every eye to read. If she had naught to do with your escape, why, then, has she turned as pale as fresh milk? Why do her limbs tremble, and why do her eyes mirror forth the fear that is within her heart? What is there to fear, if one has done nothing for which to deserve punishment?"

"I was just looking for my friend, the Professor—" I began, hoping against hope that simple honesty would convince her that I had no sinister intent. "If I had been intending to escape, I wouldn't have been prowling around the palace, but off and over the walls—"

"Enough, barbarian!" She lifted one slender hand, her voice imperious. "I have only contempt for your lies, and they will avail you naught—nay, nor will they interpose between my wrath and the guilt of the girl, Ialys, whom I loved and trusted!"

At this the little handmaiden choked a sob and fell to her knees beside the tiled pool, burying her face between shaking hands.

"Mercy, O Divine One—" she implored in a quavering voice.

The face of the Goddess softened as she stared at the weeping girl. One hand emerged from the water to touch gently the girl's head, to smooth back the locks of her complicated hairstyle, which had become disarranged.

In the very next instant—with that quicksilver, catlike change of mood I found so disconcerting—her face hardened and her superb breasts heaved with emotion.

"One whom I trusted and have given favor to has betrayed that trust," she hissed coldly. "And one to whom I offered the ultimate favor has deceived and lied to me. For crimes of such affront to the Sacred Throne, there can be but one punishment great enough!"

"And that is . . . ?" inquired Cromus with a leer, licking his lips gloatingly.

"These two shall be immurred within the Pits of Zar, to

await death in the great arena on the coming-forth of the God," she commanded.

And I must confess my heart sank into my boots. Except that I wasn't wearing any, of course. . . .

While it had proved a pretty crummy day for me, Cromus obviously found it something to write up in his diary, if the Zarians keep diaries, that is, and if he could write.

As he led us to the cells beneath the arena, he was strutting and preening himself like a peacock, shooting me smirking and malevolent little glances all the while, and in general really enjoying himself.

As for myself, I tried to keep a calm composure and an unruffled mien. It wouldn't do me any good to show my feelings, or the depths of despair in my heart, and to do so would only have pleased Cromus all the more. So I hung onto my cool and didn't even respond to his jibes.

The arena is a great amphitheatre ringed about with stone benches, and built up against the cliff-wall on whose top the palace citadel rises. The Pits, as the dungeon cells are known, lie beneath the floor of the arena, much like the ones tourists see in the ruins of the Roman Coliseum.

And I can guarantee they are just about as uncomfortable.

Chapter 27

THE PROFESSOR DECIDES

Interminable though they seemed, the sewers beneath the Scarlet City of Zar *must* end . . . this Hurok and the warriors knew; but it seemed as if they had been crawling through the fetid subterranean passageways for an abnormal length of time.

The darkness was penetrated only by the feeble, flickering rays of light cast by their torches, which burned poorly in the vitiated, moist air of the sewers. At no point along the tunnels had it ever been possible for the little band to stand erect, so they were forced to progress in a stooping position, half bent over. At times, the tunnel narrowed and the arched ceiling closed down so closely that they were forced to crawl on hands and knees.

By this time, they were all heartily sick of the experience. But there was nothing else to do but to trudge grimly on, trying to ignore the claustrophobic closeness and the stench.

After a time, the tunnels angled steeply upwards and it seemed to the Apeman of Kor that they must be nearer street level. The air became no fresher, neither did the black gloom of their surroundings lighten, but the primitive senses of the great Neanderthal told him that they were near the surface.

The others sensed it, too. No less primitive in such respects was Neanderthal than Cro-Magnon; the senses of both had been honed to keenness by the harsh struggle for survival in the jungle wilderness of savage Zanthodon.

"O Hurok," muttered Varak from ahead, "it seems that we are coming to the end of this warren."

"Hurok senses it, too," grunted the Apeman. The others felt their nearness to the street level, and their sodden spirits lifted.

"It will be a pleasure to leave these filthy holes in the

168

ground, and fight face-to-face with the foe in the clear light of day!" said Erdon with an eagerness in his voice they all shared.

"And the fresh air of the open sky," chuckled the irrepressible Varak. "Do not forget the fresh air!"

"I have almost forgotten what it smelled like, in this vile place," returned Erdon.

"Save your breath for climbing," advised the Neanderthal in his heavy tones. "It gets a lot steeper here——"

And, indeed, it did. From just ahead of their present position, the tunnel rose almost vertically, obviously almost at its end. Ascending the steep incline, Hurok blinked above, awed at the glimmer of daylight now clearly visible beyond another barred grating similar to the one they had pried free to enter the sewers.

"How do we get up *that?*" muttered Warza, indicating the vertical rise. Hurok shrugged.

"As we ascended the wall of the mountain," he growled. "We climb!"

And climb they did. Fortunately, ages of running water had crumbled and washed away the mortar between most of the great blocks of stone, and these interstices afforded them handholds and toeholds. But the throat of the sewer tunnel was slimy and very slipppery. They began to climb slowly and with much care, after falling a few times.

At length Hurok, who had taken the lead, reached the barred grating which covered the opening. So dazzled were his dim little eyes by the unaccustomed brilliance that he could make out little of the scene which awaited beyond the grating. He caught the blurred impression of noise and tumult and movement, although he could not at once make out anything in clear detail.

Bracing his splayed feet and wedging his burly shoulders against the throat of the tunnel, he clasped the iron grill in his great hands and heaved with a mighty surge of strength.

Incrustations of rust and filth groaned, cracked, flaked— gave way. The grill he thrust aside, crawling upward to hook his elbows over the brink of the opening; he emerged, cramped and filthy and sore in many muscles, to clamber to his feet and blink about him in the light of day.

One by one, his warriors emerged from the sewer to group behind him.

As his dazzled vision cleared, Hurok peered ahead and saw two things that astounded him.

One of these was the one person in all of Zanthodon whom he most wished to see.

The other was a titanic monster such as he had never seen, even in his most horrendous nightmares. . . .

Sadly watching Cromus and his bravoes march the girl and me off to face the judgment of Zarys, Professor Percival P. Potter heaved a heart-deep sigh, and returned gloomily to his work.

The elderly scientist had no way of guessing what would be the fate of his young friend, but he somberly feared the worst. Cromus he knew to be a vindictive, jealous bully and coward, who envisioned Eric Carstairs as a rival for the love of the Divine Empress of Zar. And now that same Cromus had me where he wanted me!

Hours later, during the sleep period, the old man tossed and turned, unable to still the tumult of his thoughts. My words had pierced him to the heart, showing him the frivolous nature of his scientific curiosity, and the tremendous danger which his reinventing of gunpowder presented to the world of our Cro-Magnon friends. Guiltily, he cursed his avid quest for knowledge and the fascination which Xask's challenge had awakened in him.

All that "night" he wrestled with his conscience. To stop work on the project now would be futile, for already the gun-barrels were forged and the crude black powder, although still undergong purification, was already perfectly usable. Even if the Professor stubbornly declined to continue his work on the weapons, the master smiths and artisans could carry it through to fruition without him.

After breakfast, while being escorted to the workshop, he continued moodily puzzling over the few courses of action which were available to him, striving to choose the one true action which would redeem him in his own eyes, if not in those of Eric Carstairs.

"Greetings, O wise one!" the master artisan Phorias hailed him as he entered the busy workshop. Absently, the Professor returned the greeting.

"The Goddess has requested to know how much longer it will be before the thunder-weapons are ready for use in training her troops," Phorias informed him. The Professor shrugged gloomily and muttered something or other.

"She desires to know, because on the morrow all of Zar

will be in the great arena for the Great Games and the worship of the God. . . ."

"Oh, ah?" mumbled the Professor, not really paying much attention. A gleam of malice flickered in the shrewd eyes of the bald, olive-hued artisan.

"Yes! And you should be there, as well, for on the morrow your youthful companion walks forth alone to face the God," he added suavely.

The Professor snapped out of his moodiness as if struck in the face. He stared at the other man, his old heart pounding.

"What's that you say?" he demanded fearfully. "Eric!—the dear boy? To 'face the God'—*what* God?"

"Mighty Zorgazon, the Supreme God of Zar, to whom the Divine Zarys herself is bride and sacred consort," replied the other.

Blinking rapidly, the Professor strove to recall if he had ever heard of this Zorgazon before. He knew that the Zarians worshipped a male divinity, of course, but had paid little attention to the matter. And now it seemed to the old savant that he was going to have to stand idly by and watch Eric Carstairs sacrificed to some hideous idol or other. . . .

"Get about your work and leave me to my computations," he rasped irritably, waving the other man away. With a polite smile, which was almost a mocking sneer, Phorias saluted and returned to supervising the purification of the gunpowder.

All the rest of that endless day, Professor Potter grimly wrestled with his conscience. That he must do something to eradicate the evil he had caused was perfectly obvious; exactly *what* to do was the problem.

And now, as if this weren't enough to struggle with, yet another problem had intruded. He must do whatever was humanly possible to rescue his young friend from these cold-hearted fiends. . . . He would never be able to sleep easily again, if he were forced to sit idly by and watch Eric Carstairs offered up as a human sacrifice to some Cretan idol.

Toward the end of that day, a notion occurred to him. Promptly, he dispatched a guard to request a certain object from Xask, the Empress's counselor, who was theoretically in charge of the manufacturing of the thunder-weapon.

His request was couched in cunningly phrased language which seemed, on the surface, casual and insignificant. But Potter knew the shrewdness of Xask, and feared mightily that

even this innocuous request might arouse the suspicions of
Xask and alert him to what the Professor was planning.

Fortunately, Xask was attending upon the Empress at her
court, and one of his servants complied with the request. The
guard returned with a small object wrapped in white silk,
which the Professor hastily concealed beneath his garments.

Later, as the workmen and smiths left, the Professor lingered behind, pretending to be busied with a few last details.
Once he was alone and unobserved—except, of course, for
the guards who waited at the entrance to escort him back to
his apartments—he set about his work hastily but with great
care.

Breaking open one of the wooden casks of gunpowder,
the Professor poured a gritty trail of shining black particles
on the floor. The line began at the stack of kegs which held
all of the gunpowder thus far produced, and ended at the
front door of the workroom. From there, out of direct view
of anyone at the door, the professor produced a length of tal-
low-soaked twine. One end he inserted into a small heap of
the black powder, at the end of the trail, and the other end
he extended across the floor into a far corner of the room.

The Professor had earlier planned to use just such twine in
the nature of a fuse, when he had conceived of a slightly different design for his weapons. Through experimentation, he
had learned exactly how slowly the tallow-impregnated twine
burns. Thus he knew to a nicety how long it would take for a
spark to consume the considerable length of the twine he had
stretched across the floor.

Just before leaving the workroom and locking the door, the
old man struck flint and steel.

And lit the long fuse. . . .

Chapter 28

THE GREAT GAMES

Life in the Pits of the Scarlet City was about as crummy as you might suppose it would be, and the only thing that made it endurable was the knowledge that it would soon end.

Very soon. A little *too* soon. Our fellow captives in the Pits of Zar gloomily informed us that the Day of the Great Games was almost upon us. They certainly didn't seem very happy about the fact, but then, they knew what was coming and I was still in a state of blissful ignorance.

I guess I suspected the Games to be on the order of gladiatorial combats—sort of a cross between *The Last Days of Pompeii* and the Olympics.

Shows how much I knew. . . .

There were two things, actually, that made the dungeons endurable. The other was the prisoners we were locked up with. For the most part, these were a surly, frightened bunch of Zarians who knew all too bloody well what was coming. They were a seedy lot—thieves, usurers, a murderer or two. Fat merchants caught counterfeiting or something. You can imagine the sort of scum.

The others, though, were former Cro-Magnon slaves condemned to the Games for one or another transgression, like refusing to whip a fellow slave to death or failing to kiss the dirt between some aristocrat's feet.

None of these fellows was from Sothar or Thandar, although they were the same sort—stalwart, handsome, superbly built warriors with fair skins, blue eyes, and yellow hair.

They told me that their nations were Gorad and Numitor, which were to be found far to the "south"—well, they waved vaguely in what seemed to be that direction. None of them had been born in slavery, but all had been taken captive by slave raiders who periodically descended from Zar to replenish the supplies of livestock, so to speak. None of them had

173

adjusted very well to slavery, which explained why they were here.

I liked them, especially one big blond warrior named Gundar of Gorad, who had the broadest shoulders I've ever seen this side of my old pal, Hurok. Another man, younger and with a winningly cheerful way about him that reminded me of Varak, I also made friends with. He was of the tribe of Numitor; his name was Thon.

All told, there were about thirty Cro-Magnons chained in the Pits, awaiting the Great Games. We did a lot of talking about a plan of escape, but there really didn't seem to be much point to it, although it helped us keep our spirits up.

Ialys clung constantly to my side. The daintily reared maiden felt lost, her life in ruins. I felt guilty, as she was being kind to me when Cromus caught me off guard, and because of helping me she found herself in this present predicament. So I took care of her the best that I could, and protected her from the men. Not the Cro-Magnons, of course, for they are courteous and chivalric gentlemen, for all that they are little more than savages—no, from the other Zarians. They would have heartily enjoyed a bit of gang-rape on their way to the Games. . . .

As I have already said, we didn't spend much time in the Pits of Zar, because the Day of the Great Games was nearly upon us. Just how nearly was anybody's guess, in this world without time. But that "night," just as we stretched ourselves out for some sleep, Ialys who had crept up beside me, laid her slim small hand on my shoulder.

"What is it?" I asked drowsily.

"When we awaken, Lord Eric," the girl said solemnly, "it will be to face the God in the arena."

"What God is that?"

"Zorgazon, who made the world," she informed me.

"Oh, yeah?" I yawned.

Then she said something that woke me up fast enough—

With a pitiful expression in her large, beautiful eyes, the Zarian girl whispered: "Yes . . . when we awaken, it will be to look upon the world for the last time. For in his beast-avatar, great Zorgazon is very terrible . . . and on the Day of the Games, he is very hungry . . . farewell, Lord Eric! Soon, all our sufferings will end, and we will be at peace. . . ."

Then she fell asleep, cuddled at my side.

But—let me tell you—*I* didn't get much sleep that night. "Gladiatorial games"—hah!

These people were going to feed us to a monster.

We were awakened and, oddly enough, considering what was shortly to happen to us, fed an excellent meal.

" 'The condemned man ate a hearty breakfast,' " I quipped. The Cro-Magnons regarded me solemnly.

"Sorry, fellows," I said with a feeble grin. "Joking helps to keep my spirits up!"

Thon of Numitor glanced at me with a twinkle in his eye, but said nothing. My huge friend, Gundar, somewhat more grim and stolid and less mercurial than the Numitorian youth, looked at me with a certain admiration.

"It is a brave man who can jest in the very jaws of death," he rumbled. I winced.

"Please, Gundar—do you *have* to say things like that?" I protested. He shrugged.

"The jaws of Zorgazon are mighty jaws, Eric Carstairs. I have attended my Zarian owners in this arena many times, and have seen the monster—worshiped."

"Let's change the subject," I begged. "Ialys is losing her appetite.

The girl smiled wanly, but said nothing.

In a little while they assembled us into ranks, and marched us out into the daylight. We walked across a sand-strewn floor about the size of a football stadium, and to every side rose tiers of stone benches crowded with gaily dressed Zarians in their holiday finery. They cheered and hooted as we emerged blinking into the light.

"Looks like a full house," I muttered to myself, trying to muster a bit of swagger into my stride.

The guards halted us in the center of the arena, and left hurriedly, closing the thick-barred gate to the Pits behind them.

In a curtained box, Zarys lolled in a glittering harness of gilded leather studded with flashing gems. To one side of her, Xask reposed, favoring me with a slight smile. To the other, Cromus sat, looking me over with a gloating, malevolent grin.

I could cheerfully have throttled him.

Beneath the royal box, a very huge door swung slowly open on ponderous hinges of solid brass, revealing the yawning mouth of a black cavern.

I put my arm about Ialys's trembling shoulders.

Out of the gate stalked Zorgazon.

The crowd gasped and quailed. The Zarians in our little band fell to their knees, wailing and pressing their brows against the sand in abasement. The Cro-Magnons stood tall and proud . . . and, like myself, empty-handed. Not that any weapon this side of a howitzer would have done any good.

For the God of Zar was a gigantic tyrannosaurus rex!

As the host of Sothar approached the entrance to the pass which led to the Scarlet City, Garth eyed without comment the gigantic dragon heads positioned to either side, hewn from the living stone of the cliffs. I had seen those very heads when Raphad and his troop had led us into the pass, and remembered that Xask had humorously referred to them as "very good likenesses" of the God of Zar. Which indeed they were.

Suddenly, Garth threw up his hand, halting the march. For his keen eyes had seen his scouts hurrying through the foothills, running with all fleetness, as if being pursued.

"Archers! Bend your bows," rumbled Garth, hefting his long spear and loosening his war axe in its sling. The bowmen nocked their bows and held them at the ready.

The first of the scouts came running up to where Garth stood in the forefront of the Sotharian host.

"What have you seen that impels you to return in such precipitous haste, Mordan?" inquired the Chief.

The scout panted for a moment, recovering his breath. Then he spoke.

"Withdraw to better ground, my Omad!" said Mordan hurriedly. "A great host approaches down the pass which leads through the mountains. They will be upon us sooner than you might suspect!"

Garth nodded, lifting his aurochs horn to summon the chieftains. When they were assembled, he gave rapid orders. The host withdrew to a large knoll which stood amid the grasses of the plain some little distance away. To his practiced eye, it looked to Garth to offer as much advantage as could be expected in such flat land.

His warriors encircled the knoll in a triple ring of men. They locked their long, kite-shaped shields together, for all the world like the Vikings of olden time, and crouched behind them so as to offer the least possible target to their approaching adversaries.

Atop the knoll, Garth and his personal guards stood waiting for whatever was coming to emerge from the mouth of the pass.

There was a long moment of stillness, as if the very world of Zanthodon held its breath in suspense.

Then the ground seemed to tremble slightly, as if to the tread of ponderous feet.

"Dragonmen, my Omad!" one of the guards said alertly. From a little distance away, the Minoan prisoner, Captain Raphad, smiled slightly. He, too, recognized the heavy tread of the feet of the thodars.

In the next moment, a host of running figures burst from the pass to flee into the plain.

At their very heels came stalking along the giant forms of the mounted dinosaurs.

"Who are those warriors in front of the line of beasts?" rumbled Garth, shading his eyes with one hand.

"I recognize one of them, at least, my Chief," observed a keen-eyed warrior. "Is it not—? It is! It is. . . ."

In the next instant, the eyes of Garth of Sothar widened incredulously, and his bearded jaws gaped in a startled cry.

Chapter 29

ZORGAZON!

The thing was as big as a house. Quite literally; it stood on enormous legs towering as tall as a three-story building. In contrast to its huge hind legs, the forelegs were small but sinewy, and armed with hooked claws like wicked sickles. Its hide was leathery, pebbled rather than scaled, of a brown-greenish hue on the back which faded to muddy yellow on the chest and belly. It stank like a pit of squirming snakes.

Its hideous head seemed to be all gaping jaws packed with fangs longer than cavalry sabres. Under the shelving of its brow, scarlet eyes blazed—soulless, unwinking orbs filled with ferocity and wild hunger. I have little doubt that the Zarians had starved the brute for days to give it sufficient appetite—*for us.*

As it came clambering up the runway into the arena, Zarys rose to her feet and saluted her husband and consort with a regal gesture. The tyrannosaurus seemed to recognize her, for as she lifted her arm in salute it threw back its horrible head and gave vent to a screeching cry like a tugboat's steam whistle.

Then, with an eloquent gesture, she drew its attention to us. That ghastly, grinning head lowered; we met the impact of those mad scarlet eyes.

"Zorgazon!" she cried imperatively.

"Zorgazon," moaned the vast throng as with one voice they hailed their monstrous God.

With a ponderous stride that shook the ground, the giant reptile came stalking across the arena toward us. We stood our ground, the Cro-Magnons and I, and I held little Ialys tightly against my chest. But the Zarian captives broke and ran, squealing.

Zorgazon peered down at them curiously, fang-bristling jaws agape, saliva dripping in slimy ropes from its scaly chin.

"Shrieking men were plucked into midair
and popped into that vast maw."

Then one huge splay-toed foot lifted and came down on a
whimpering cluster of Zarian thieves.

They . . . *squelched*.

The foot lifted, dripping crimson. I shuddered and bit my
lip.

Beside me, giant Gundar gripped my shoulder. "Steady,"
he rumbled.

I nodded grimly.

Zorgazon broke into a loping stride. Half-bent, it snatched
with those sinewy little grasping forelimbs. Shrieking men
were plucked into midair, popped into that vast maw like
peanuts.

Zarian after Zarian it snatched up and gobbled down. It
seemed to be ignoring us, perhaps saving us for last, as a
diner samples the hors d'oeuvres first, while savoring the approach of the main course.

Then those blazing scarlet eyes glared down at us, and our
turn had come.

There was nothing we could do to defend ourselves. But,
then, bare hands were every bit as useless against that titan of
the Dawn Age as swords or spears would have been. Its leathery hide was tough—impenetrable.

The shadow of Zorgazon fell over us, like the shadow of
doom.

And then the world went crazy!

The ground jumped under our feet. The floor of the arena
shuddered, then tilted crazily. Stones fell clattering from the
nearer wall of the arena. Women screamed.

We looked up, dazed.

A boiling cloud of inky black smoke enveloped the upper
works of the palace citadel. Whirling, seething black smoke
shot through with streaks of furious crimson.

A deafening explosion shook the very air. For a moment,
all I could hear was my ears ringing. Momentarily deaf, I
could not even hear the uproar as the crowd went mad, and
men came leaping down the tiers, running headlong for the
exits.

Another explosion, louder than before. Again, the arena
floor rose to slap against the bottom of our feet. Gundar and
Thon glanced at me, shaken.

"What is it?" one of them gasped.

"Who knows? Or cares? Run for it—"

The second explosion took off parts of the palace roof, and felled one tower. It fell slowly, like a falling tree, except that it came apart with dreamlike slowness as it fell, disintegrating into a shower of stone blocks that pelted down across the arena in a deadly rain.

Zorgazon did not like the explosion, or the sulphurous stench of the drifting black smoke. He threw back his hideous head and screamed his challenge.

A mass of falling masonry came whirling down, and caught the tyrannosaurus aside the head. He staggered sideways, shrieked again, dark red blood trickling down his working jaws.

At that impact, the dinosaur went crazy. He headed for the grandstand and plowed into the stone wall. It came apart as if built of children's alphabet blocks. Seats crunched, people scattered. *Splat—splat!* went his little forepaws, as he swatted the crowd, leaving wet red marks that had been men.

Huge as he was, Zorgazon could not break through the solid stone construction of the arena. So he swung about, and swiped with his thick, long, heavy, kangaroo-like tail. It thundered against the side of the arena like twenty bulldozers, and even the stonework had to give. Screaming like fury, he began kicking and punching his way through the side of the arena.

I got one glimpse of Zarys, frozen, standing alone in her box. Her gorgeous face was white with unbelieving horror—white as death.

Then the framework of the box gave way and her slim, proud form vanished as the awnings fell.

Gundar slapped my shoulder. We turned and ran for it. I grabbed up Ialys, flung her across my shoulder. The thirty-odd Cro-Magnons and I headed for the nearest exit.

Along the way we found a couple of guards and relieved them of spears, swords, tridents—whatever.

Another explosion ripped the palace apart. The crackling of flames shooting up from burning buildings was very loud in our ears; soot and hot ashes fell about us in a stinging black snowstorm.

Suddenly a huge, hairy form heaved itself up in front of us.

"A Drugar!" yelled Thon, and made to fling his spear.

"*No—*" I shouted, knocking his arm aside. For in the same instant I saw the recognized Hurok of Kor, and he knew me.

"Friend," I panted. Thon glowered, but subsided. Beyond

Hurok I saw Varak and several others. I wondered dizzily what they were doing here, and how they had managed to find their way, but there was no time for that now. Zorgazon was going crazy, tearing the arena apart, and stones the size of Volkswagens were thumping down all around us.

We found the exit and dived into it.

The streets around the burning palace were a howling madhouse. Zorgazon had come this way, and houses had been smashed flat under the tread of his ponderous feet. People, too, if you can call smears of wet redness people. Villas had been kicked apart, luxurious gardens trampled into mud. And, everywhere, ashes were falling, falling.

We headed for the stone causeway across the inland sea. Just about everybody was heading in that direction, too, and nobody tried to stop us or even bothered to notice us. I saw men waddling along, their arms loaded with bric-a-brac and rolled-up tapestries, women weeping, but hanging on for dear life to their jewelry boxes, scared-looking kids hugging jointed wooden dolls.

Zorgazon was somewhere up ahead, towering above the rooftops, howling like a fire engine. He swatted at a tower and it burst apart in a shower of bricks. He kicked in the side of a mansion as a man might kick in an egg crate; it folded in upon itself, collapsing in slow motion.

We ran, dodging through side streets and narrow alleys to avoid the crush of jammed, stampeding humanity that choked the main boulevards.

I tripped over a fallen pillar and went down on my face. Hurok caught me by the shoulder and lifted me to my feet like a rag doll, while Gundar paused to scoop up the limp form of Ialys, who had fainted sometime during the nightmare of the streets. He threw her over his shoulder and kept on running, as if the girl weighed nothing.

Suddenly, out of the veils of falling ashes and smoke and whirling sparks, a scrawny, gleeful figure appeared smack in front of me.

"*Professor*—!"

"Eric, my boy," he panted. "I've been chasing after you for blocks—"

I cocked a thumb back at the wreckage of the burning palace, high on its hill atop the city.

"Did—you—do—*that?*"

He nodded happily. "Yes, I'm afraid Xask and Cromus will not have their rifle platoons, after all," he chuckled.

"Professor . . . you amaze me," I said helplessly.

"And that's not all," he breathed. "I managed to carry off a little souvenir."

He whipped a silk-wrapped bundle from under his smoke-blackened garments and thrust it into my hands.

It was my .45 automatic!

We got across the bridge and headed straight for the pass. The sooner we shook the dust of the Scarlet City from our heels, the happier we would all be.

There were plenty of other fugitives crowding the causeway, but all they wanted to do was to put the breadth of the inland sea between themselves and their God run amok.

Nobody tried to stop us, or even bothered to notice us. It was weird, almost like being invisible. You would think that thirty-five blond Cro-Magnons and a huge, hairy Neanderthal would have attracted *some* attention from that crowd, but no.

At the top of the pass we paused to take a breather. Along the way we had all picked up plenty of weapons, and it felt good to be armed again. It also felt good to be able to stop running and sit down for a while.

Then Hurok grabbed my shoulder in a hand the size of a catcher's mitt.

"Look, Black Hair, they pursue us," he grunted.

I turned and my heart sank into my boots.

Down the length of the causeway came the Dragonmen, twenty strong, mounted on their immense loping thodars.

On the lead beast rode Zarys of Zar in her glittering golden harness. Directly behind her rode Cromus, his face flushed and angry, red murder in his eyes.

They were not escaping the burning city, no, not them. They were set to hunt down the fleeing slaves and prisoners who had caused all of the commotion in the first place.

White-faced, her superb eyes flashing with fury, Zarys rode like the avenging goddess she was. And, of the two Gods of Zar, I cannot say which of them was the more dangerous and implacable, Zarys or Zorgazon!

This day she had worn that sparkling wig of spun gold that made her so closely resemble my lost, beloved Princess. How beautiful she was—how glorious!

And how deadly. A woman—a queen!—scorned and rejected by the man to whom she had offered her love, and by whose bold connivance her splendid city now lay in blazing ruins.

To have earned the undying enmity of such a woman is not the sort of thing that lets you sleep easy of nights. . . .

I looked at Hurok and Gundar. They looked at me.

Then we . . . *ran.*

Chapter 30

RAPHAD STRIKES

When Garth of Sothar saw the band of running men who emerged from the mouth of the pass and came pelting down the slope onto the plains, he frowned in puzzlement. Most of them were tall, strong, blond Cro-Magnon stalwarts like himself, but none of them was known to him. From their accouterments and the way they braided their long hair, he guessed them to be mostly warriors of Numitor and Gorad.

What it was that they were running away from he did not at once see. For, suddenly, to his complete astonishment he began to recognize the faces of men whom he knew among the throng of strangers.

There in the very forefront was Eric Carstairs, with mighty Hurok of Kor at his side! Puffing along behind them he spied the scrawny form of Professor Potter, who still clung gamely to his dusty pince-nez spectacles and his battered and travel-stained sun helmet.

About these, like a guard, were the missing warriors Varak and Ragor, Erdon, Warza, and Parthon—men of Sothar and of Thandar all.

Then there emerged into view the giant forms of the thodars, each with its armed rider seated between the shoulders and straddling the massive column of the reptile's long neck.

But nowhere did he espy the form of his lost daughter, Yualla. . . .

With arms folded upon his mighty breast he waited as we came up to the knoll where his warriors were arranged for battle. I burst through the line, bearing the limp form of Ialys in my arms, Gundar and Thon and Hurok at my heels.

"Garth!" I called, "these men are friends—former slaves in Zar—let them join your ranks!"

Handing the unconscious form of the Zarian girl to the solicitudinous arms of his mate, Nian, who bore her off among

185

the women, Garth issued the command. Reluctantly, the ranks of Sothar parted to admit the warriors of Gorad and Numitor among them. The Sotharians eyed the newcomers suspiciously, and were stared back at with grim truculence.

I joined Garth on the height, and together we observed the huge forms of the lumbering thodars as they came out of the pass and drew up in a vast half-circle. There wasn't much that we could do to defend ourselves against the vengeance of Zarys, but at least we could go down fighting. I felt sorry that Garth had shown up just in time to have to face with me the Dragonmen.

"I perceive, Eric Carstairs, that again you have been making a few enemies," the Omad observed with somber humor. I grinned.

"A few," I admitted.

"May I inquire into the cause for this pursuit?"

I shrugged. "Well, we left the royal palace of Zar a flaming wreck, and the arena of the Games has been knocked apart, and a considerable portion of the city lies in ruins. . . ."

He nodded solemnly. "I suppose that is enough to make an enemy of anyone," he commented. "If you were a slave in Zar, did you encounter therein my child, Yualla?"

I blinked, this being the first news I had received that the teenaged girl was missing. Reluctantly, I admitted that I had not seen her.

"Or Jorn the Hunter?" Hurok rumbled questioningly at my side. Again, I shook my head negatively. Garth sighed, then straightened.

"Then she is lost," he said heavily. "Time enough to mourn our dead when this present circumstance is over."

I gave him a surprised look. "There isn't much even you and your brave men can do against the Dragonmen," I protested. He shook his head with a slight smile.

"We have faced them before, and won," he remarked, gesturing to where Raphad stood between tall guards. I was amazed to see the little Captain who had first taken the Professor and me prisoner, but there was no time to ask what had been going on.

For just then Zarys lifted her gleaming lance in a royal gesture of command, and the huge, lumbering thodars began to advance upon our position.

Among the Dragon-riders I recognized the angry red face of Cromus, but nowhere did I see Xask. It would have been perfectly in character for that sly devil to have concealed himself in time to miss this expedition—if, in fact, he still lived.

And if I had been Zarys, I certainly wouldn't have felt comfortable leaving the Scarlet City behind, with Xask there. . . .

But there was no time for these thoughts right now: we had a bit of fighting to do, and, I thought, a bit of dying, too.

With slow and ponderous strides the great thodars advanced upon our position across the grassy plains. Their long, snaky necks reared high above us, and their long, thick tails dragged through the trampled grasses.

You couldn't have brought down one of monster brontosaurs with a hand grenade, much less a javelin or an arrow, or even my precious .45. Realizing this, I couldn't understand why Garth seemed so confident.

As they came near, the High Chief of Sothar reached into his fur garment and withdrew a circlet of sparkling, reddish-silver metal, crowned with a dully glittering crystal.

This he placed upon his brows, and turned to face the advancing Dragonmen with a kingly frown upon his majestic features.

The Cro-Magnon doubtless believed the circlet to be a magic charm. The technology of the uncanny telepathic receptor was naturally beyond his primitive experience. But he had nothing to lose and everything in the world to gain by testing its strange powers. . . .

In the forefront, the Divine Zarys saw and recognized the circlet, and frowned, her furious expression changing to one of slight uneasiness. . . .

She almost raised her hand to halt the advance, to call a parley. But then she saw the Professor and me among the others and her face hardened again into an expression of vicious hatred.

With a wave, she signaled the charge—

At that precise moment, Garth hurled the full power of his iron will against the advancing reptiles.

With every atom of strength his disciplined mind and strong body possessed, he willed the beasts to halt in their tracks. And the will and mind of such as Garth, monarch of Sothar, was much more powerful than was the will of the Dragonmen, their inner strengths vitiated by the decadence of their enervating pleasures and by the soft pamperings of urban life.

The monster saurians came to a halt.

Wild-eyed, Zarys tugged at the reins, pummeling the sides of her gigantic steed with her heels. But she might as well have kicked a stalled locomotive, for all the reaction she got. Consternation and surprise flickered in the features of Cromus and the other Dragon-riders when they discovered that they had unaccountably lost control over their mounts.

Never before, in their experience, had such a thing happened. Frowning in concentration, they hurled their wills against that of Garth, commanding their steeds forward to trample and crush the blond barbarians.

But the beasts did not move, although they stirred restively, giving voice to bewildered and plaintive honkings.

A huge grin split the somber visage of Garth of Sothar. Merriment twinkled in his hawklike eyes.

He hurled another mental command at the giant reptiles. The stream of his thought waves, augmented and tightened into focus by the strange power of the circlet, broadcast his mental command into the tiny brains of the placid saurians.

The beast which Zarys rode turned, its long neck curving, small, snake-like head questing.

Jaws opening, it reached down and plucked the fear-frozen form of Cromus out of the saddle of the next beast. The head rose high into the air, the tiny figure of Cromus kicking and fighting in panic between its jaws.

The brontosaurus was a herbivore, not a meat-eater. Its jaws were huge and powerful, but they were not lined with fangs as are the jaws of a predator. Thus it did not eat or swallow the hapless Minoan; it didn't have to.

It *tossed* him.

Like a flimsy doll, the tiny form of Cromus whirled up into the air and came down to thump against the plain. And that was that, as far as Cromus was concerned.

Garth turned his attentions to the next thodar. Its long, serpentine neck curved down, but this time the Dragon-rider managed to leap out of the saddle in time to avoid meeting the same doom as Cromus. He fell, sprawling on all fours in the long grass. Picking himself up, throwing aside trident and helm, he went sprinting off in the direction of the pass. Better to face a burning city and a God amok, than stay here and be tossed about like a child's doll, were his obvious thoughts.

Freed one by one of their riders, the huge reptiles were

lumbering off amid the plains in search of fresh water or succulent grasses. Zarys, too, slid off her mount and vanished in the direction of Zar before Garth could turn his attention to her. I was glad to see her escape death, and hoped that I had seen the last of her.

Raphad paused only long enough to realize that Garth had seized control of the thodars before making his move. The wily little Minoan officer had planned his next action. He had found a smooth, heavy stone amid the grasses, which he had hidden in the folds of his cloak. Now he drew it forth and, turning swiftly, struck one of his guards in the head with the rock. The man fell and even as he toppled, Raphad whirled and struck down the other guard.

Then he threw himself upon Garth before anyone could stop him, and the unexpected impact of his weight bore the surprised High Chief to the ground.

I yelled and made a grab at the Minoan, but Hurok was there before me. His huge balled fist rose and fell; with a sickening thud he broke the neck of Raphad with a single blow. The corpse kicked, then slid face-down into the grass.

We bent to help Garth to his feet, but then we drew back in consternation.

For in the split-second before Hurok slew him, the wily little captain had whipped a bronze dagger from Garth's scabbard. *And had plunged the blade into his heart.*

WHAT HAPPENED AFTER

We met there in council on that knoll amid the plains, the chieftains of the host of Sothar and my friends and myself, to decide what must next be done.

It was a strange, sad ending to an amazing day full of surprises. I've seen victory plucked out of the very jaws of defeat before, as the saying goes, but this was one of the first times I ever saw triumph followed so swiftly by stark tragedy.

The one redeeming factor was that, somehow, miraculously, Garth had survived the assassin's blade. The sharp knife had missed the mighty heart of the jungle monarch by a hair's-breadth, but it had missed it and the great artery, too.

But Garth lay on the very threshold of death, and he could not be moved. With hands as steady as those of a surgeon, Professor Potter gently withdrew the blade of the dagger from Garth's chest. Nian, the monarch's mate, stanched the flow of blood with tender care. The wound was packed with healing herbs, and bound tight.

There remained a chance that Garth would live, but only a chance. In time, perhaps, his body would heal itself. He was a magnificent physical specimen, with the vigor and stamina of two men packed into his powerful frame, and, although a man of middle age by the standards of the cavemen, a strong man in the full noontide of his prime.

For the moment, the tribe of Sothar must be led by the will of the chieftains. For Garth had left no son to succeed him to the Omadship, only a daughter, the lost Yualla, whom we all believed to be dead somewhere in the mountains.

"We cannot remain here," argued Parthon. "There is no source of water, and no trees from which to fashion huts to protect us from the elements."

"We could withdraw to the south, where the jungle stands

at the end of the plains," suggested Varak. "There we would no longer be at the mercy of wind and rain."

"*And* be at the mercy of the first prowling grymp or drunth or vandar that comes along," sniffed the Professor, who always liked to put in his two cents.

"We could move into the foothills and perhaps find caves there," suggested one of the chieftains, a warrior named Thorg.

"And be all the closer to Zar," I pointed out. "And closer to its vengeful queen."

My friend Gundar of Gorad nodded grimly. "The Divine Zarys in her unappeased wrath will mount another expedition against those who defeated and disgraced her," he promised. "I have been longer in the Scarlet City than have you, Eric Carstairs, and I understand the folk thereof more completely. The Witch Queen will never rest until she has dealt out fitting punishment to us all. . . ."

"Pooh!" scoffed the Professor, brandishing the circlet which he had retrieved from the brows of Garth. "If she sends thodars against us, we shall fend them off as before, with *this!*"

"And if she sends an army?" inquired Hurok in his heavy, deep tones. The Professor flinched and wilted.

"The legions of Zar are not to be despised," said Thon of Numitor, for once without his cheerfulness.

"I think the wisest thing to do would be to go back across the plains again and try to get together with the tribe of Thandar," I said. "That way, we can put as much distance as possible between ourselves and the Dragonmen and double our fighting strength, if it comes to fighting. . . ."

"How soon can the Omad safely be moved?" inquired Gundar of Numitor of the Professor. The elderly scientist shrugged, then pursed his lips thoughtfully.

"Our friend Garth is a very strong man, brimming with superb health," he mused. "Holy Hippocrates, but I should say—if he continues to rest and mend—within six or seven sleeps. Then we might bear him, very slowly and carefully, in a litter. With frequent stops, of course."

And so it was eventually decided.

One week later, the host of Sothar decamped from the vicinity of the knoll and moved off slowly toward the northwest. There, across the width of the great plain, somewhere the tribe of Tharn of Thandar wandered, searching.

There, somewhere beyond, on an unknown island amid the steamy waters of the Sogar-Jad, my lost Princess, Darya of Thandar, remained in captivity with the cruel Barbary Pirates.

Would Garth survive the assassin's cowardly blow, and would we ever find Yualla or Jorn or my beloved Darya again?

Only time would tell.

I marched at the head of the host, my thoughts dark and my heart heavy. At my side went my new friends, laughing, lighthearted Thon of Numitor and huge, powerful Gundar of Gorad. At my back marched the faithful warriors who had come through so many perils to rescue me—Varak of Sothar, and Ragor and Erdon of the Thandarians, Warza and Parthon.

And the best and chiefest friend I had yet made during all of my adventures in Zanthodon the Underground World— Hurok of Kor. He had become a leader of men during his search for me, and a chieftain of Cro-Magnon warriors. He had found within his loyal and faithful heart the courage and wisdom and leadership that one might not expect of a Neanderthal, perhaps.

Sometimes, in dire adversity, men break. Other men, however, pass through the fire and emerge strong and tempered, like steel passing through a smith's forge.

And thus had been the fate of my old friend and comrade-in-perils, Hurok of the Stone Age.

THE END

But the Adventures of
Eric Carstairs in
The Underground World will continue in
DARYA OF THE BRONZE AGE,
the fourth volume in this new series.